KILLER DOMES

AND THE

CHOSEN ONE

A debut novella by Gibbo Gibbs

© 2019 Gibbo Gibbs

Killer Domes and the Chosen One is a work of fiction. The characters, incidents, situations, and all dialogue are entirely a product of the authors imagination or are used fictitiously and are not in any way representative of real people, places or things.

Any resemblance to persons living or dead is entirely coincidental.

All rights reserved.

No part of this publication may be reproduced, stored in a retrieval system or transmitted in any form or by any means electronic, mechanical, photocopying, recording or otherwise, without the prior written permission of the author except in the case of brief quotations embodied in critical articles and reviews.

Chapter 1

"Load file, Maz, cathedral one, version one."

In a sudden assault to the retina, a bright and spectacular three-dimensional image of a cathedral flashed up in the otherwise pitch-black void. Its staunch spire, flanked by a pair of pinnacles, rose from the fore of its deep and ancient stone frame; the structure was a magnificent achievement, for something formed by merely primitive hands. The old world fascinated Maz, and she loved nothing more than to scour the data banks for gems such as this. Ideas rushed through her mind for restructuring the interior; with so much space inside, she would divide it into levels, with spiral staircases to climb and slides for a swirling descent. The possibilities inside Canvas were almost limitless. In a virtual reality design platform, with many categories to choose from, citizens passed through life distracted from the restrictions they faced in their physical world.

The avatar of her best friend Hap stood to her right: a keen, yet somewhat useless, organic designer. Maz couldn't remember Hap ever working on an inanimate design project like this, which made his enthralled reaction to the cathedral a little unconvincing; beneath his rather stylish black tricorne pirate hat, he gawped open-mouthed. But the problem stood there - the thick black beard, hanging from his mouth down to his midriff and ruining an otherwise handsome young face.

"It's incredible," he said.

Maz moved her attention back to the grand structure, yet left some space in her peripheral vision to spy on her friend. Hungry to understand the unknown, and with a growing suspicion towards aspects of her environment, she recently made Hap the subject for a little minor experimentation.

All citizens followed a regular rest and reboot procedure, but Maz believed this affected others differently to her. Reboot couldn't only be waking from rest but must be something more. And for this reason, she persuaded Hap to skip a few cycles, for her to observe any changes in his behaviour. In the short term, this wouldn't be considered illegal, and she believed it might even affect him positively ... or so she hoped.

The pirate's attention turned slowly towards the leather breeches of her avatars lederhosen outfit, or possibly her unclothed legs. This kind of strange behaviour never occurred until Hap skipped reboot, and this intrigued Maz.

Hap turned away suddenly. "So what did people do here?" he asked, as his attention returned to the cathedral.

"It's another temple, for god worship," Maz answered.

Hap nodded as though it were obvious in hindsight. To locate the most beautiful structures of the old world, Maz had always achieved the best results by searching the data banks for places of worship. And not only the buildings lured her: the stories, the bizarre rituals, the fact that unproven deities inspired such glorious creations and intriguing cultures. Maz sensed this becoming an obsession.

"Was it for the god with the elephant head?" Hap asked, raising a hooked hand to the structure.

"No, it's a Jesus temple," Maz answered.

She ignored his stupidity regularly. In a life of scarce companionship, she found Hap to be the least strange of the strange folk, which marked the end of her tiresome search for a friend. With a mind hard-wired on animals, attempts to expand his horizons and encourage him away from organic design had proved unsuccessful. His intelligence appeared limited, which would certainly prevent him from ever reaching master creator status.

Hap pouted his lips and tapped them with his hook.

"Jesus ..." he mumbled. "The flying man with a cape?"

"No," said Maz. "The one who walked on water, then flew away after he died ... without a cape."

"Ah!" said Hap with a quick nod. "Yeah, long hair, flowing like a cape from his head while he's soaring through the clouds. I think that's how I got them confused ..."

Maz zoned out from the babble and continued to form a picture in her mind's eye. One of the levels inside the cathedral would be a stone-wall maze, with awakened gargoyle scares and gemstone-encrusted golden artefact rewards. Another level would be a floor-is-lava scenario, with net ladders and complicated climbing structures, positioned over harmless, yet deep and dreadful, flame coloured goo-pits. Maz often wished it possible for her and Hap to experience her projects in the physical world; the ability to explore recreated places with exciting modifications would be so much fun. She began to contemplate the idea of tiered infinity pools along the rooftop when an irritating sensation on her legs interrupted her thoughts. She bent down, tutting with discomfort and swiped at them, causing her plaited hair to swing.

"Close file," said Hap. He released a soft chuckle, but the smirk behind his big beard fell the moment Maz looked up.

"What on earth was that, Hap? Another useless organic design project?"

"It's not useless. I'm quite pleased actually," Hap answered, in a panicked, defensive tone. He lowered his head, concealing his expression with the point of his hat.

With a squashed side-mouth, Maz awaited the poorly considered details, which from her experience of Hap, would be due at any moment. "Well?" she said, growing impatient.

Hap cleared his throat, revealed a determined face, and raised his hooked hand to shake conviction into his words. "So ... you know the interesting insect from the old world, the mosquito?"

Maz sighed. "Disgusting, not interesting," she answered. "They sucked blood from humans and spread diseases."

"Exactly. Very interesting," Hap said with a grin. "Well, I've improved it to be a more efficient predator."

Their creative ideas differed significantly, but for the sake of their friendship, Maz allowed him to waste her valuable time. "Go on," she said with a sigh.

Hap appeared saddened by her tone, but a moment later he raised his shaking hook again and proceeded to explain: "So ... to make it a more efficient predator, I've introduced genetic code from the ant, trading wings for a protective exoskeleton and pheromone trail capabilities."

Maz shook her head and walked away, in her thoughts.

"My super mosquito can then lead a trail of super mosquitoes through a tiny space to a discovered source of blood – such as a sleeping human." With a proud smile, he awaited Maz's response.

"What about nectar?" she asked.

"What *about* nectar?" Hap answered.

"Well if you'd paid full attention to the data banks, you'd know that only female mosquitoes sourced blood as protein for egg production. They ate nectar from plants like other flies, but now you've taken away their wings to reach them, *stupid*."

Maz didn't mean to insult Hap so frequently, but he often deserved it. On this occasion, however, he appeared smug. "What?" she asked.

Hap took a deep breath. "Well ... if *you'd* paid full attention to the data banks, you'd know that ants *also* ate nectar – same as mosquitoes. They just got their *protein* from aphids and dead insects so they can eat nectar as normal, thank-you very much." He jerked his neck, then started to dance, humming a celebratory tune.

A dangerous pressure rose from Maz's neck to the back of her head, and negative emotions teased the illegal threshold. She learned over time how to suppress these feelings, but sometimes this still proved a challenge. With teeth clenched tight, she turned to the cathedral and took a slow, deep breath, while twisting her hanging plaits. She relaxed her shoulders and cleared her mind, allowing reasoning to resurface.

"So," she said. The one word killed Hap's moment. "What you've done here is created what is essentially just an ant, which sources its protein from human flesh instead of dead insects ... and *you're* a human." She could've stopped there, but Maz always struggled to tolerate stupidity. "Redesigning a species," she continued, "so it more efficiently draws nutrients from *your* species, while delivering disease in the process ... *that,* Hap, is species suicide. If you gave me a hundred segments to think of a worse idea, I'd struggle."

The corners of Hap's mouth quivered behind his beard.

"You're wasting your time," Maz added. "You had much better ideas before you started meddling with animal hybrids."

Maz excelled in every design category, so whatever she submitted would return high ratings. Hap, on the other hand, didn't achieve the same level of success. He would complain he only enjoyed organic design, despite having the potential to score higher in categories such as sound design and visual design. Maz liked Hap, but if he continued to ignore her advice, she might be forced to hunt down a less annoying, more intelligent friend, returning Hap to the solitary life of the strange folk.

"Right, I'm going to rest and reboot now," said Maz. *Could skipping again do him harm?* she wondered. *No.* "You seem fine, so don't bother. Start a new project, a different category this time."

"But–"

"You're not breaking the law Hap, don't reboot yet," she insisted. "I'll meet you in the garden in nine segments. I look forward to seeing you without that horrible beard."

Hap grabbed his beard with his non-hooked hand as everything went black. Maz no longer stood beside him, but she remained in his thoughts. He stared into the dark void as a negative emotion weighed him down. Skipping reboot again sounded like a bad idea; he needed the rest, and something didn't feel right.

"Avatar menu, face, beard, remove." He let out a long sigh. "View avatar."

A young man appeared before him; a young man in a *costume*, unconvincing. The beard made the pirate authentic. He tried a variety of fierce expressions, but it didn't help. He *needed* the beard, but he didn't want it now, because Maz didn't like it. *I don't understand,* he thought, confused.

"Canvas menu, new project." A grid of bright buttons lit up in the void. He read them aloud as he perused his options. "Visual Design, Sound Design, Game Design, Inanimate design, Organic Design–" It was his favourite category. With so many smart ideas, one of them would soon impress her.

Chapter 2

Nine segments passed, and Maz's eyes shot open as reboot kicked in. She focused on the sensations in her body, desperate to unlock their secrets. A beaming smile, holding no invitation, had sprung from ear to ear, and a great rush of energy swirled through her until she was more awake than she needed to be.

"Eject!" she said, and the pod around her popped open, dropping her naked, hairless body to a squatted position on the floor of her bare, pure white room. She extended her tired legs and raised an arm to protect her sensitive eyes from the displeasing radiance trespassing through the transparent front surface. She turned from the light and with little enthusiasm, made her way towards the rear wall, stretching and waggling each limb, bringing them to life. She rubbed the sore skin around the metallic fixings on her spine, grabbed her customary long white tunic from its hook and slung it over her bald head. She shuffled back a few steps as she shook it into place. "Menu," she said, staring at the wall's white surface.

A tall stack of coloured rectangles appeared in her augmented reality vision, and she nodded a little as she moved between options. The colours represented her choices of post-reboot sustenance, and she'd unlocked many premium flavours as rewards for her projects. At this rate, she would almost certainly earn them all and reach master creator status within her lifetime.

"Select." A hidden hatch shot open in front of her, revealing a tall beaker of thick green liquid, tailored to her specific nutritional requirements. She clasped her hand around its smooth, cold surface and raised it to her lips. Hap would be waiting in the garden, so without hesitation, she drank until her lungs throbbed for oxygen. After some rushed breaths, she wiped the bubbles from her lips with the back of her hand and returned the almost-empty beaker to the hatch.

She passed beneath her pod, which loomed over her like a giant open mussel shell of the old world ocean. The mechanical claw inside appeared keen to snatch her up again, so she hurried to the transparent front wall and poked it, alerting it to her presence.

DING-DING! DING-DING!

The surface didn't slide open. Instead, an alarm bell summoned her from behind. Maz turned with a sigh and tramped back to the hatch, tutting as she retrieved her pot of lotion from behind the beaker. Hap didn't need lotion; she was special apparently. She slapped a handful on her bald head and massaged herself from head-to-toe, reaching awkwardly beneath her tunic until her whole body was sticky and uncomfortable. "There you go, satisfied?" she muttered, as she returned the pot to the hatch, which answered her affirmatively by vanishing into the wall. She crossed the room again, and the front surface slid aside this time, allowing her to step onto the narrow ledge outside.

Maz perched on the fifth floor, her legs swaying as she waited for a moving platform from below. She readjusted her vision to the broader depth perception as she gazed ahead at the community centrepiece: the printer column, bursting up through a central courtyard and rising to the apex of the impenetrable dome structure which contained the citizens, protecting them from the fires of the apocalypse outside. The column marked the centre of their circular environment, from where everything surrounded in rotational symmetry.

Maz lived in the south block, Hap in the east, and a north and west building completed the circle, four of them in total. These residential structures, with sides ten rooms high and ten wide, each had a path leading straight to the central courtyard. The rest of the town circle was lawn, green and pristine, with some large shrubs, bouncy and immaculate spheres, but not much more.

The platform arrived, and Maz stepped on. She staggered as it departed without warning and as her wobble centralised, it crept to one side before beginning a casual descent. Maz resided on the front of the block, allowing her a clear view of the town centre, providing warning of any unwanted interactions. Thankfully, on most days, the area was unoccupied. Most citizens would only leave Canvas for nutrients from their hatch, but sometimes they bravely emerged, lurking around the printer column with their creative boasts or boring small-talk. As the platform descended, to Maz's utter disappointment, she counted six or seven today, *all* on her route.

The platform met the pale, grey surface with a gentle thud and Maz stepped her bare-feet onto the soft, synthetic material. Without a moment to waste, she proceeded along the south path towards the central courtyard, trying to ignore the fact that ahead of her, on a bench to her right, the first two citizens sat waiting to disrupt her crossing. She focused forward, keeping her attention on the printer column, which pale grey like the path and about the same breadth, towered high, as though inviting her to walk to the sky.

Maz approached the occupied bench and shot a glance; she hated her curious mind at times. The two women sat at opposite ends, speaking to their feet with bald heads bobbing up and down agreeably. She couldn't help but eavesdrop as she passed.

"My last visual design project got rated seven point two."

"I expect mine will rate higher. Would you like an invitation to view it?"

"No. Would you like to see mine?"

"No. But you should see mine."

Hap would be waiting, so Maz picked up her pace. She couldn't waste any time with lesser creators and their substandard projects. With an average rating of 9.2, she cared nothing about human opinion. Other citizens were so irritating, posing a severe threat to her biochemistry, blood pressure and patterns of thought. She preferred her interactions in small doses – and her small dose was Hap.

The path became courtyard, and chattering voices arose from a huddle on the opposite side. Maz concealed herself behind the printer column, where a blinking notification flashed up in her lens implant, drawing her attention to the square hatch on the wall. She ignored this as always; it was never anything interesting. As a child, she had wasted many segments sat here, cross-legged and gazing up. Not only for the notifications but being small enough to climb inside, she imagined being transported to a magical world underground, to a secret civilisation who sent things to the dome. Now a young adult and twice the size, the opportunity had passed. This was probably for the best, as however tempting, the most likely of outcomes would have been a slow and painful death, in terrifying darkness, somewhere unknown.

Maz stepped cautiously around the column. She ran her fingers along its smooth, spotless surface and peered towards the north residential block. Behind the structure, the taller plants of the Vegetation Zone formed a pleasant narrow ring of uninhabited nature which circled the town, partially concealing a dark-green wall, failing in its deep forest illusion.

Behind each block, paths crossed the grass to penetrate this greenery. And through the gateways beyond, the walls folded over, forming a network of corridors to a hundred unmarked doors. Known as the Outer Zone, this area filled the space between the town circle and the dome's thick and robust shell which marked the boundary of Maz's existence. She had never encountered another citizen in these passages; nobody else could cope with being so far away from Canvas – or reboot more likely. From a young age, she would sneak into the Outer

Zone to explore, never finding much of interest, until that is, the day she discovered her garden.

Maz leaned further around the column to spy on the north path. Five citizens stood huddled in a deep conversation, and one of them boasted a full head of bouncy blonde hair. To encounter a citizen more than once in the dome would be a rare occurrence. Most would loiter until their peculiar behaviour intensified, then would rush back to their pods, never to be seen again. The exception to this would be the dome leader; with responsibilities exceeding Canvas, she would often float around the courtyard with her silver decoration of privilege hanging from her neck and shoulders, painting the atmosphere with positive energy.

Bel was her name, and Maz was quite fond of her. Calm and thoughtful, her citizens were her family, and she was always caring and empathetic, even to those with low Canvas rating. A bench-sitter once spoke of her ability to heal people by merely waving her hands near them. This apparent knowledge of subtle electromagnetism, however, was more likely a mere fantasy, a conversational icebreaker, no doubt.

Despite Maz's admiration for Bel's superior status and Canvas history, the last thing she wanted right now was a tedious conversation with strange folk. With steely eyes on the gathering, she crept out from the column and edged forward, extending her legs into soft, stretching strides towards the north path. The group profusely gossiped as she approached. *Please don't see me*. She held her breath, rolling each step from stiffened toes as she passed them, and soon, the pleasant sight of a clear path welcomed her. A smile broke through, and the air from her aching lungs escaped in a long, silent breath. *A successful crossing*, she thought as she hurried north, but then a gentle, yet enthusiastic voice startled her from behind.

"Maz ... Maz, my lovely."

Maz turned as Bel broke away from the chattering huddle, waving with one hand and lifting her long tunic with the other, shuffling over with a glow of excitement on her face. Maz couldn't help but relax as the warming, motherly energy stepped into her space.

Bel clasped her hands together as she arrived. "Maz, my angel. So wonderful to see you." She leaned closer, bouncing her fused hands with enthusiasm and asked: "Now I *must* know your thoughts."

Maz waited for her to continue, but her leader watched her, expectantly, until the sparkle left her eyes.

"Are you okay, Maz?" she asked.

Maz nodded. "Yes, I'm fine," she answered. "What do you mean?"

Bel scrunched a smile and delivered a delicate laugh. "You didn't read it, did you? Silly thing," she said.

"Oh!" said Maz, remembering the notification. "Sorry, I must have missed it."

"Missed it?" Bel seemed amused. "You walked straight–" she shook it off slowly. "Never mind. A baby boy will arrive at the printer soon. Isn't that exciting?" She gestured her head towards the huddle nearby. "It would be lovely if you joined us, dear. We're trying to decide between the names Bim, Bam, Bom or Bob. Will you please join us?" She gazed at Maz pathetically, waiting for an answer.

I'd sooner chew out my kneecaps than join that conversation, Maz thought after taking one more look at the bundle of bobbing bald heads.

"Sorry, Bel," she answered politely, "but I must get going. I'll see you soon." She turned and marched at the north block with purpose. There would be no more interruptions today.

"Oh ... Maz. Wait, one more thing!"

Maz stopped and turned reluctantly, masking her frustration with a smile. Bel caught up a few steps and leaned in with a sincere whisper and an expression of grave concern.

"Maz, dearest. Could you please have a quiet word with Hap for me?"

"Sure, what about?" Maz asked.

"Well ..." The dome leader paused for a moment, then leaned in further. "I'm sensing negative energy, and I suspect ... well, I suspect he may have reduced his reboot frequency."

Maz raised her eyebrows, trying to appear surprised.

Bel turned to check the other citizens were still out of earshot. "You remember the danger of negative energy, don't you?" she asked.

"Yes, of course," Maz answered without hesitation. Then to remind her leader she was now an adult and didn't require a child's education, she recited the verse: "No negativity. Like the plague it does spread, until all fall down dead."

Bel returned a proud smile. "Good," she said. "No negativity. Like the plague it does spread, until all fall down dead. Now please, check what's wrong and let me know, will you?"

Maz nodded. "Yes, I'll speak to him," she said, and she hurried towards the north block before the overwhelming feeling of guilt could bubble to the surface.

"Thank you, my dear," Bel yelled from behind. "Oh ... and keep up the wonderful work in Canvas!"

The path forked, wrapping the building. Maz couldn't help but gaze into the ground floor rooms as she passed on the right side; the pods were all clasped shut as the citizens worked hard on their inferior project ideas. At the rear corner, the grey surface beneath her feet crossed the grass, leading to a gap in the Vegetation Zone, a gateway to the Outer Zone. After passing between the tall plants, the path seamlessly became a corridor as the purest white walls and ceiling closed in around her. It reminded her of her room, but much longer, with something beautiful waiting at the other side.

Maz took the familiar route to the garden and considered Bel's words. Hap would never snitch on her, but maybe it was time to suggest a reboot – she may have pushed him too far.

Chapter 3

SNIP ... SNIP ... SNIP-SNIP.

Beyond the garden gateway, the grey path expanded to form a terrace, where a defiant fist propped up Hap's head as he waited for Maz, gazing from a bench across a large lawn towards a lonely, ancient tree. Behind the eruption of green leaves, the dome's lucent outer wall rose over him, peacefully humming as it harvested the fires of outside to fuel a perpetual daytime in the dome. Flowers of every colour decorated the garden's rim, reaching out with their intense aromas, and petals which they liked to pick off and scatter. When Maz first brought him here, she announced it as perfect, because it was the furthest escape from the strange folk of the town.

Low green shrubs surrounded the terrace, and an Assistant Synthetic Human, or Ash-bot for short, was busy making minor adjustments with a pair of pink plastic scissors. *SNIP ... SNIP-SNIP ... SNIP-SNIP ... SNIP.*

The helper robot had a gloss-white finish, and over this, it wore the same tunic as the humans, as its body shape was considered human-like enough that unclothed it could prove a potential hazard to the citizens' legal biochemical levels.

Hap groaned and sat up straight. He tried rubbing the blurriness from his vision, but it didn't help. The Ash-bot paused its mindless activity, and the rear-skull window to its electrical identity rotated, presenting a vacant, genderless face. The eyes were dark caverns, with optical lenses expanding and contracting inside.

For a moment they observed each other, but the deadlock broke as hurried footsteps approached from the corridor behind. The Ash-bot turned away to resume its duties, and Hap forced a smile as Maz reached the bench, breathless as she settled.

"Sorry. I got delayed near the printer, are you–" she stared at her friend. Not only did he look terrible, but to her amazement, some light, fuzzy patches of hair had sprouted around his lips and on his head.

"What?" Hap asked. His eyes were puffy and half closed.

With the Ash-bot nearby, Maz remained calm for the moment. "Nothing," she lied, with her trust of the dome further withered.

"You saw Bel in town then?" she asked.

Hap's face drooped with his body. "No," he answered. "I haven't seen her for ages."

SNIP-SNIP ... SNIP ... SNIP-SNIP-SNIP.

For a standard of garden already more than adequate for two visitors, the trims were slight and unnecessary. As a child, Maz never questioned the passive existence of the Ash-bots, but that was beginning to change.

"Hap, you must rest and reboot, okay?" she said.

"But I've waited–"

"I'm sorry," she interrupted. "Just a short rest, then we go back. Alright?"

The snipping ceased, and the Ash-bot crossed the courtyard with an awkward spring in its step. Once it disappeared into the corridor, Maz snatched Hap's head with both hands.

"Argh, what are you doing?" he complained.

Maz shook and twisted his head as her frantic hands harassed him. "Incredible!" she said with a gasp. "Your hair is growing since skipping reboot. You need to stay out!"

"But you–"

"Seriously, Hap. This means Bel doesn't reboot. She isn't strange, so rebooting must make people strange! Isn't this exciting?"

"But I–"

"Don't you want to be less strange?"

She released his head, stood from the bench, and leapt to the grass with a rare burst of joyful energy. "Let's go to the tree," she said.

"But I don't feel too good," Hap said, grasping his head and wincing with discomfort.

"You're fine," Maz reassured him. "You can lie down over there."

The old, wise one, she thought. From the first time she laid eyes on the tree, she imagined its early years and the things it must have seen before the dome rose to consume it. Thick and wrinkled, its veins swelled from the earth, immortal in their hunt for nutrients. The old world relic pulled at her with a mysterious magnetism.

A groan sounded from behind as Hap stood, then they treaded over the pristine lawn, with tunics waving in their stride.

"I've been wondering," Hap said as they strolled. "How did humans make the cathedral that size without any machinery?"

"Amazing, isn't it?" Maz answered. "Have you come across the Great Pyramid in the data banks?"

"Not a great one, I don't think," Hap answered, rubbing his head. "I remember the wrapped-up cats and the gods with animal heads."

Typical Hap, Maz thought. He had a talent for diverting any conversation to the subject of animals.

"But did you know," she asked, "when they mummified humans, they poked a long hook up the nose to pull out their brain?"

Hap laughed with grinning repulsion but quickly glanced back at the tree. "Something moved," he said, raising a pointed finger.

Maz squinted. "Where?" she asked.

Hap walked a few steps ahead, and then a whisper blasted out from the tree.

"Idiots, come here!"

Maz's heart started thumping, and her head became tense. *How dare they,* she thought. *It's my garden.* There was only one solution; she must banish the citizen by committing aggression, warning them never to return. Hap would be her witness; he would lie for her. But she remembered, *don't do anything in anger*, and she inhaled deeply, forcing herself to stay calm. It was a bad idea; she should be more like Bel. They must turn around and leave the garden, forgetting about this encounter. The hidden citizen would soon hurry back to Canvas.

The voice spoke again, louder this time, in a restrained yet determined plea. "I need your help. I'm in the tree!"

Maybe he's trying to leave? Maz wondered, with forced optimism. *That might be why he needs our help?* With Hap close behind, she began circling, scanning every branch for a shiny bald head peering down. She stumbled over a thick root as they reached the other side. Nobody appeared to be hiding among the leaves, but as she opened her mouth to call out, another blast of the voice frightened her.

"In the tree. Not on the tree!"

Sturdy root collars supported the base of the tree's broad torso, and between two of these was a hatch, expertly camouflaged with mud, moss and grass. An arm from the cavity beneath raised the flap higher, and a set of piercing eyes stared up from the shadows, where a man crouched like an ambush predator waiting to strike. He wore a shirt with rolled-up sleeves, black to match his hair. Memories of Maz's childhood fantasy came flooding back. *The world beneath the dome!*

"Sit down and stop staring," the man whispered aggressively. "The Ashers could be watching."

Stunned by his assertiveness, they dropped to the soft, trimmed grass and glanced around in an unconvincing attempt to act natural.

The stranger climbed back out, lowering the hatch behind him, and started brushing his hands on his black trousers, muttering complaints about the state of them. He rested his back against one of the root collars, fidgeted until comfortable, and swept his hair back as he turned to introduce himself. "You can call me Mitch for now," he said. "Did any Ashers see you?"

"Ash-bots?" Maz asked. Her words shook with her thumping heartbeat.

"Obviously. You idiot. What else would be spying on us?"

A slight surge of anger failed to materialise through Maz's rushing thoughts and fascination. This Mitch, whoever he was, seemed fierce with purpose. He knew things she didn't; she could sense it immediately.

"Do you live under the dome?" she asked.

Mitch screwed his face at her, but then leapt to his feet and rushed over to Hap, who flinched like a coward as the visitor lunged at him. They tussled for a moment on the grass until Mitch gained possession of Hap's head.

"This is great," he said. "Your hair is growing. You're avoiding reboot!"

"Get off!" Hap moaned, pushing the man away.

Mitch released him and wandered back to the hatch, grinning with satisfaction. "Follow me. You can become a disciple," he said. He clapped his hands and rubbed them together. "I've got important things to show you."

"What about me?" asked Maz. "I want to become a disciple."

Mitch crouched, then he turned with disapproval as he raised the hatch.

"Not you," he said. "Go back to your pod."

"But I'm not like the others!" Maz protested. She crawled closer; there was no chance Hap was going on an underground adventure without her. "I told him not to reboot," she pleaded with him. "I want to learn the secrets of the dome."

Mitch had already ducked into the tree to escape her approach, but in response to her words, he shuffled back out, looking surprised. "Interesting," he said, lowering the hatch. "Then it seems we have something in common."

"What can you tell me?" Maz asked, with a burst of excitement. "Tell me everything. I want to know it all."

Mitch grinned, with a scheming glint in his eyes. "Perfect," he said.

"I don't understand," Hap moaned.

"I need your help," Mitch said to Maz. "I'll pay you with secrets. How does that sound?"

"Yes!" she answered without hesitation. "We'll help."

"Good," Mitch said. "Follow me."

He raised the hatch again and ducked under, grinning profusely. Once in the burrow, he held the flap up for Maz and beckoned her inside.

Maz turned to Hap, who was still clasping his shaken head with a puzzled look on his face.

"You can reboot soon," she said with a weak attempt at sympathy. "But this man needs our help."

Nothing unusual ever happened in the dome, and Maz feared she would grow bored of the garden one day. Her body was trapped, but her mind reached far. And today, at long last, she faced the prospect of adventure. A disciple spreads teachings; she knew that much. But what would be taught? What secrets would he reveal? Her heart raced with anticipation.

Chapter 4

Beneath the dome, Maz's palms met with damp earth as she felt her way through the darkness. With Hap close behind, she crawled forward until her hand slipped through a hole and she fell to her elbows, causing the ground underneath her to bend.

Mitch spoke up from below. "Jump down, it's not high," he said.

Maz lowered her feet first and perched on the flimsy edge. She slid through until she fell, and her hands and feet thumped down on the cold metal surface beneath.

The area lit up, and she found herself in an open space, surrounded by a grid of narrow beams with squares large enough to fall through sideways. The ground directly beneath her appeared safe, but things promised to be more challenging from here.

Mitch slung a flickering lamp over his arm. "Hold the ceiling for balance," he said, as Hap thudded down behind them.

Above them was a wire mesh, cut and twisted away to allow access to the burrow. At the edge of the grid, Mitch reached up and clawed his fingers in; then with racing hands, he strode across the nearest beam with ease. The orange glow from his lamp revealed a larger island on the other side. "Hurry up," he said. The lamplight enhanced his boastful grin.

Maz gripped hold of the wire netting, which seemed to cut into her fingers as she steadied her wavering legs and stepped forward with caution. The bottomless pit distracted her as she placed her feet, but she soon reached solid ground.

Hap was surprisingly close behind, with eyes now bulging and alert. "Is there a different way back?" he asked after leaping to safety, panting as though he'd held his breath the entire time.

"Nope," Mitch answered. He wafted them into a burrow in a nearby wall, which appeared to lead upwards.

"Another garden!" Maz said as she returned to the surface. She crawled forward, admiring the mess at her knees: crispy fallen leaves, broken twigs, tangled weeds; the complexity fascinated her. The Ash-bots had somehow neglected this area.

Hap crawled beside her, rummaging in desperation. "Profile ... profile," he muttered.

Mitch finished slapping his trousers and rolled down the sleeves of his shirt. He rested his hands on his hips and stopped to observe Hap's strange behaviour.

"Profile!" Hap said again, becoming agitated. "I can't bring up its profile!"

"What are you doing?" Maz asked.

"I've found a real beetle," Hap answered, as he repeatedly pounced, ripping open the undergrowth.

Maz was about to suggest that lack of rest was beginning to play with his mind when something unexpected occurred; the air moved against her face. She raised her head to meet an audience of trees and became dizzy; this deeper forest was no illusion. The dome wall towered behind her but emitted no light. "It can't be," she whispered. She leaned back and gazed upward to infinity.

"Secret number one good enough for you?" Mitch asked.

Maz responded with a slow nod. At a young age, in Canvas, a video taught her that human greed destroyed the old world, causing the people to perish from drought and famine. A group known as The Elite pooled together the remaining wealth and resources into a panic of technological advancement and managed to escape the planet moments before the sea of flame. The Elite's mission was to establish a new colony in space, but with the risk of failure being so high, they created the dome to protect what may become the last of the human species. But this was no blazing wasteland.

"Hey," said Mitch, clapping his hands and breaking the trance.

Maz rose to her feet in the forest clearing, but Hap was back in the burrow, peering out with fearful eyes.

"What are you doing now?" Maz asked.

"Look!" Hap answered, pointing past her.

Staring at the sky had affected Maz's vision, but as she blinked at the trees, the blurriness began to solidify. A huge man was bounding through the forest towards them, with heavy, crunching steps.

"Come on," Mitch yelled, with his back turned to the approaching giant.

The man stomped closer. He was as grey as the dome paths, and with mechanical elbow joints beneath the short sleeves of his black, buttoned shirt. *A synthetic human,* Maz realised.

Mitch shook his head at his followers, as the heavy footsteps halted and a stretching smile loomed over him. The robot's eyes were human-like but showed no emotion, making the huge smile unconvincing.

"Hello, Mitch, my friend!" the figure bellowed in a dunce tone.

Mitch turned to greet him. "Logan. There you are!"

The robot let out a moronic moan of excitement. "This makes me feel happy, Mitch, my friend. I was experiencing the emotion of worry."

Mitch hugged an arm around Logan's thick frame, presenting him to his followers. "I was finding us some new friends, Logan. Look," he said, pointing them out.

The robot smiled from Mitch's shoulder down to his finger and then noticed them. "Hello!" he boomed, stepping forward. "My name is Logan. How does it feel, meeting a new friend?"

What a strange Ash-bot, Maz thought. She'd never seen one of these.

"He asked you a question, idiots," Mitch snapped. "Or was it too difficult?"

They panicked positive remarks and introduced themselves.

"How did you get a big Ash-bot?" Maz asked.

Mitch stared at her with a reddened face. "If you call him an Asher again, I'll feed you to the ants," he said.

"I'm a person!" Logan boomed with enthusiasm.

"This is nice, but I need to go back soon," Hap whispered. "My body is so weak."

"No, not yet," Maz whispered back.

"But–"

"Not yet."

"But I don't feel good, and I think my lenses are damaged."

"Problem?" Mitch asked.

Hap alternated exaggerated winks. "I think my lens implants are broken," he said. "I couldn't bring up the beetle profile, and now there are stains in them."

Mitch rolled his eyes. "Why would the Elite scum profile the things they abandoned?" he asked. "And your lenses aren't damaged, you probably looked at the sun. You seem like the kind of person who would do something like that."

Hap continued winking.

"Are you coming then?" Mitch asked, looking at Maz.

"Yes, of course!" She grabbed Hap by the arm. "Let's go," she whispered. "We need to learn more."

Chapter 5

The temperature outside the dome was hotter, but not uncomfortable. Leaves rustled in the light breeze, accompanying the chirps and cheeps in their veiled performance among the trees.

Maz wished for the soft paths of back home as her bare feet crunched over the spiky twigs. She gazed through the forest, desperately wishing to glimpse an old-world structure, but only nature presented itself. Her mind overflowed with questions, but Mitch demanded silence. *"No more secrets until you earn them,"* he'd said, which frustrated her. Maz wanted to understand everything, and she didn't like waiting.

Hap was still alive. The encounter with a real beetle must have been the highlight of his life so far, so his attention swayed in every direction, in late response to mellow hoots, and distant cracks and rattles.

"How does it feel to walk through the forest, new friends?" Logan asked, turning his smiling head as he trudged along in front of them.

"I'd like to see more creatures," Hap answered.

"I'd like to see an old-world structure," said Maz, "but–"

"You answer with your thought patterns, friends," Logan interrupted. He stopped and rotated his broad frame, causing Maz and Hap to halt abruptly. "I want to know your emotions," he said in a saddened tone, smiling down at them.

"Happy, joyful, excited?" Mitch yelled. He leapt up a low hill to the right, which the group had been walking beside for some time. "Too difficult for you, is it?" he asked. His chin rose as he scanned the forest ahead.

"You are feeling disappointed," Logan stated.

"No, not at all," said Maz. "We are feeling happy."

"But your answers indicate a high probability of disappointment and a low probability of happiness," Logan calculated.

Mitch wandered back along the raised ground and descended with a few rapid stomps. He stopped beside the robot, patting him on the back. "Don't worry, Logan," he said. "You're learning well. These two are just not very smart."

Maz battled a rising tension with a long, deep breath. She would prove her intelligence to him soon.

Mitch swung out a hand to bring her attention to the raised ground. "You see this mound?" he asked. "These are perfect for navigation."

The hill stretched as far as Maz could see through the trees, ahead and behind. Mitch awaited a response, but there was nothing to be said; it didn't interest her.

"*This* is an old-world structure," he informed her. He turned and continued walking, with Logan resuming his stomping pursuit.

There was no denying Logan's calculation now. From a young age, Maz imagined what could still stand among the fire and ruin beyond the dome walls. Flames incinerated the animals and plants, but not the structures of stone; the skeleton could remain: the fossil of the old world. Leaving the dome reignited this dream, yet the mound beside her was *not* that dream.

"Wait!" she shouted, jogging past Logan with negative emotion threatening to surface. "Every old-world structure is now a mound?" she asked, aiming an aggressive finger at the hill.

"Any containing metals, that could come under strain *and* were not maintained, yes, they are now a mound," said

Mitch, marching more hastily than before. "But the domes are different. They are active prisons, living machines," he added.

"What do you mean?" Hap called out from behind.

"But not all had metal," said Maz. "What about the ancient buildings of stone?"

"That's enough for now," Mitch said.

"No ... no, it's not enough for now," Maz said, angrily. "If there's nothing out here, why are you leading us further from the dome?"

She stopped. It was time for Mitch to do some talking.

Hap stepped up beside her, let out a quiet groan, and then squatted to the forest floor. "Can we do this another time?" he asked, pinching his eyelids. "I think I should rest and reboot now. I'm tired, and my arms feel weird, they keep shaking." He opened and closed his hands, as though trying them on for the first time.

Mitch returned with a disgruntled sigh. "Look ... I don't want to spoil all the surprises," he said, "but I'm taking you to a village where you can rest. Have you ever tried illegal sleep, you know, sleeping outside your pod?"

Hap's eyes lit up.

"A village?" Maz asked. "There's a community out here?"

"We're working on it," Mitch answered with a grin. "Would you like to meet the old-world survivors?"

"Yes!" Maz cried.

"Yes, but illegal sleep first please," said Hap, returning to his feet.

"Great. But you both need to promise me something," Mitch said. "Don't ask them any foolish questions, alright? The end of the old world is a sensitive subject for them."

"Why?" Maz asked.

"Isn't that obvious?" Mitch answered. "The Elite abandoned their ancestors and–" He froze still and turned his head. "Shhh." He grabbed them both by their tunics and lowered his knees, pulling them down with him.

"What is it?" Hap asked.

Mitch rolled up his sleeves. "Lay down."

They pressed their chests to the dirt, staring into the forest ahead. Silence followed until Mitch turned his head. "Oh dammit," he said.

The broad and obvious Logan still stood behind them, smiling to himself obliviously.

"Get down, Logan," Mitch said, waving a frantic hand at his companion.

In a rather clumsy manner, the robot dropped to his knees. He leaned his body forward, strangely not making use of his arms, until the balance shifted and his face slammed into the dirt. "I'm down, Mitch, my friend."

"What is it?" Hap mumbled. His eyes were now closed, and his mouth squashed against his folded arms. The anticipation of real creatures seemed to be the only thing preventing his total collapse.

"Ants," Mitch answered with disgust.

Hap raised his head and propped himself on his elbows. "Where?" he asked.

Maz spotted one, moving eagerly and erratically near her right hand. *It would struggle with a bunch of needles stuck out from its face,* she thought, with the memory of Hap's foolish project returning to her mind. This ant posed no threat to the group, so she tried to establish the direction of Mitch's stare. Then she gasped. A trail of unclothed Logans were crossing the distant forest up ahead. "Logans!" she said.

Logan rose to his knees again, and a lump of moss fell from his head as he turned it. "Yes, Maz, my friend?"

"They are *not* Logans, they are *Ants*," Mitch said with an angry whisper. "They scavenge like ants, and they move in a trail like ants. We call them *Ants*."

"Sorry–"

"And Logan is *not* an Ant," he hissed. He turned again to the robot. "Get down!"

CLUNK!

Logan's prompt plummet introduced his head to a rock, startling the others. "I'm sorry," he said.

Hap returned to his folded arms, but Maz froze. The Ants had stopped and turned, and like a pack of animals stalking their prey, they peered through the trees, smiling in their search for the source of the sound.

"Don't ... move ... a muscle," Mitch whispered.

"No problem," Hap mumbled into his arm.

Maz kept her head down and trembled as she awaited Mitch's next instruction.

"I'm crawling forward," he whispered eventually. "There's a gap before the next mound. If we crawl through, we can follow the next one crouching on the other side."

Hap raised his head briefly. "Can you come back and get me later?" he asked.

"No," Mitch answered, and he turned to Maz. "Once I reach the gap undetected, I'll make a signal. If they don't notice me, they shouldn't notice you either."

Maz nodded, and then he turned to Logan.

"Logan, wait here until everyone has gone, then meet us at the village ... and make sure you're not followed."

"Yes, Mitch, my friend. I am sorry for what I did."

"Just stay away until it's safe. I don't want you drawing any more attention, alright?"

"Yes, Mitch, my friend."

Mitch dragged himself forward in near silence, as Maz watched nervously, wondering how he'd selected this idea as his best. If the Ants were dangerous, a wider diversion made more sense to her. But Mitch didn't seem like the patient type. He reached a distant tree, positioned himself behind, and after brushing off his trousers, he beckoned her to follow.

"Hap," she whispered. "We need to crawl forward."

Hap groaned. "Already?" he asked. He propped himself on his elbows and squinted at the forest ahead.

"Bye, friends," said Logan, smiling as always.

Maz repositioned her arms and slid forward, attempting to mimic Mitch's technique.

"Wait," Hap whispered, grabbing hold of her leg.

"Hap, we need to–"

"No, wait, look."

Mitch hadn't realised, but the Ants had seen him. He beckoned his followers again.

"Don't move!" said Maz, waving to signal the threat.

They all smiled towards the tree, with the closest Ant leaning forward, tilting its head, anticipating another glimpse of the target.

Maz waved again, but she was too late. Mitch beckoned them once more, and the Ants took off, bouncing with enthusiasm as though it were a game. The moment he heard, he leapt to his feet, sprinted at the gap, and then the chase disappeared.

Logan fumbled to his feet and turned to face his new friends. "Mitch asked you to follow him, friends," he said.

Maz pushed Hap's sweaty hand from her leg as she stood. "But we can't help him, Logan," she said. "What will they do if they catch him?"

"Do not feel worry, Maz, my friend," the robot replied. "Mitch has a faster running speed."

"How far away is the village?" Hap asked wearily from beneath them.

"Two more mounds then the tunnels," Logan answered.

Hap groaned with disapproval.

Maz brushed at her tunic, clearing some of the leaves and dirt. "It's okay," she said. "We'll just follow you instead."

"Not possible, Maz my friend," said Logan. "Mitch's orders."

"But we need to hurry," Maz said. "He never said not to follow you."

The response startled her, as the robot replied with a recording of Mitch's voice: *"Logan, wait here until everyone has gone, then meet us at the village ... and make sure you're not followed."*

"Everyone has not gone, and nobody can follow me," Logan said.

"That's ridiculous," said Maz, and she kicked Hap's lifeless body. "Get up. We're going back."

Maz marched away with tension flaring. She'd learnt many things today, with one being that talking robots were programmed to be equally as irritating as talking humans.

"Shut up," she shouted in response to Hap whinging about illegal sleep. She then glanced over her shoulder, and the stupid robot was still standing in the same position, smiling at them.

At a further distance, she waited for the faltering Hap. "Get behind a tree," she said as he approached.

"Why?" he asked.

Maz chose the broadest tree and leaned her body against the bark's rough surface. "Stay still," she said as Hap did the same.

A few moments later, she peered out, and Logan was bounding off into the forest. "*Now* we can follow," she said.

Chapter 6

"I think he went down here," Maz said, pointing as they approached a gaping hole in the earth, framed by uneven ground. She stared into the abyss, having no idea what could exist beneath the forest, but Logan had disappeared, and this was large enough to accommodate him.

"Are you sure he went this way?" Hap asked, keeping his distance.

Maz lowered a foot to the first step. They were heavily eroded and continued beyond the furthest reach of sunlight. "I'm not sure," she said, stepping back up.

"Are you scared?" Hap asked.

Maz let out a laugh which was louder than anticipated. "No, of course not," she said, and she began a slow and cautious descent.

"Me neither," Hap said, and he followed.

The steps were sturdy enough, and as the light faded around her, Maz ran her fingertips along the damp wall for guidance. By the time her feet reached level ground, the passage had become as dark as the pod she'd left behind, so sploshing her toes slowly through the patches of shallow cold water, she hoped to avoid collision with obstacles unseen. She inhaled the crisp, fresh air, and the drips of water echoing in the still silence calmed her, luring her deeper.

"It's happening," Hap whispered. "The darkness is doing it."

"What are you talking about?" Maz asked.

"Illegal sleep," Hap answered.

"You're not asleep," said Maz. "You're walking, and you're talking."

"No, seriously," said Hap. "You don't understand how nice the feeling is. I could lie down right ... can I lie down right here?"

"Just keep moving," Maz whispered.

They continued their careful steps until the passage veered to the side, and a faintly illuminated T-junction appeared up ahead. As they approached, Maz lowered her hand from the wall. She squatted, shook her now slimy fingertips in the shallow water, and then dried them on her tunic.

"Left, or right?" Hap asked.

Maz reached the end, and it became clear that the faint orange glow flickered from the passage to the right. It was likely that Mitch stashed a lamp at every dark location, so with heightened confidence, she chose the obvious route. Only a few moments later, to her relief, familiar voices rose from up ahead.

"... thought you were my best friend, but you're just a big idiot, aren't you?"

"That makes me feel sadness, Mitch, my friend."

"Now I have to go back to that damned tree. What if nobody visits it again? You've ruined the mission!"

"I'm very sorry, Mitch, my friend."

As Maz and Hap stepped around the corner, Mitch span around with a seething red face; but his anger quickly dissolved.

"Friends!" Logan bellowed with his usual smile.

Mitch let out a sigh of relief. "Come on, let's go," he said, and he turned and marched away with his lamp raised high to conquer the darkness ahead. Maz hurried past Logan to avoid walking in his shadow, and then Mitch continued speaking as though the recent shambles had never occurred.

"Right," he said, "so I'd better explain a few things before we reach the village."

"Are we nearly there yet?" Hap asked as he stumbled to catch up.

"Almost," Mitch answered. "If I tell you their history, can you promise not to ask them any questions?"

"Yes, we promise," Maz answered, eager to learn more.

"Good," said Mitch. "Now, as you know, when The Elite left to colonise space, they didn't take everyone."

"That's right," said Maz. "They created the dome to protect us, in case the mission failed."

Mitch laughed and then blew air through his tightened lips. "It was never going to fail. Anyway ... this area was once a vast metropolis, a final stronghold of human civilisation as the rest of the planet fell. It was home to the original elite, numbering in the tens of thousands at the time."

Maz used her best knowledge of that era's architecture to construct an image in her mind. It was fascinating that the forest had once been a hive of activity, yet she was deeply disappointed that nothing remained for her to see.

"Once all the spacecraft were built and equipped," Mitch continued, "and the heat outside became unbearable, a complex selection process then determined who would depart and who would remain on the surface, under the ... the dome. The planet was then abandoned, leaving most of the city's population to die."

"Wait ... what?" Maz asked. "The dome didn't teach us that."

Mitch turned and held the lamp to her face. "And you trust the dome, do you?" he asked. "I thought you were following me because you didn't?"

He was right. Maz didn't trust the dome, but the deceit now reached far beyond her original suspicions. Mitch turned and resumed his steady march, and she hurried to keep up.

"The truth about what happened was passed down in their folklore," he continued. "You could imagine the riots that would've occurred when the spacecraft abandoned the city. So, to protect the dome, a virus was released to clear the city's population."

Maz couldn't believe what she was hearing. Was her community precious enough to justify the murder of tens of thousands of innocent people? With the population destined to burn anyway, leaving the dome to protect the last of the human species on earth, then yes, maybe it was that valuable.

"Many scientists worked in the restricted area north-east of here," Mitch explained. "They would have been aware of the plot, and probably putting it into effect." He coughed into his fist and continued: "Two of them decided to smuggle vaccines outside of the wall, administering them to a few local families. Hardly enough to prove they had a conscience, but anyway, those families survived the virus. So now you understand why we don't talk about it. The ancestors of the Skullkrakat were unwanted by The Elite and were chosen to die. Understood?"

"Skull crack?" Hap yelped. "You go ahead, Maz. I'm stopping here for illegal sleep. Wake me on your way back."

Maz turned and yanked him up by the armpit before his knees could reach the ground. "Don't be such a coward," she said. "We're almost there."

They soon entered what Mitch advised would be the final passage, and he went on to explain that the tribe's main symbol was the skull, and the chieftain's name was Krakat. The combination of these words would form their identity under the current leadership – which seemed to reassure Hap, somewhat. The ancestors of the Skullkrakat survived by adapting to live underground where it was cooler, surfacing only to hunt and forage under the moonlight. With the city's subway as a starting point for a tunnel network, over many generations they extended their reach as far as mining sites in the south and freshwater aquifers to the east, and once the planet was clear of human infestation, the earth miraculously healed itself and an abundance of life soon returned to the surface. Despite this, however, the majority of the Skullkrakat still refuse to experience daylight. The sun is their enemy, and it would take someone special, and highly intelligent, to convince them otherwise.

Maz entered a daydream, imagining how her whole life could have been leading up to this. Bel said she was special, and she was aware of her superior intelligence. Mitch didn't know it yet, but it would be her; she would be the one to convince the Skullkrakat otherwise.

"Come on, idiots!" Mitch yelled from up ahead. "We're here!"

Maz snapped out of her thoughts to find her pace had slowed, or that Mitch had sped up to avoid any further conversation.

"Speed up, friends," said Logan from behind.

With a burst of enthusiasm, Maz then jogged forward, following the flicker of Mitch's lamp around a corner until she faced the glare of firelight, and a pair of eerie shadows reaching across the passage walls towards her. She waited until Logan and Hap arrived behind, and she stepped forward hesitantly, into the warm, thicker air.

"Come on, stop wasting time," Mitch yelled, turning around to beckon their haste.

A pungent, musty aroma filled Maz's nostrils as she edged closer to a pair of large, muscular figures who stood blocking their path.

"Gakit, Tamak, move your damned spears!" Mitch ordered.

The guards didn't move. Each wore the outsider black shirt and trousers and had long hair tied back behind aggressive faces that snarled past the humans to a bigger concern.

Mitch tutted. "Gakit, Tamak, move your damned spears, I haven't got time for this."

Without taking his menacing eyes off Logan, the first man moved his tall, glistening blade, and then the other copied.

"Thank you," Mitch said, and he passed between them.

With a tight grip on Hap's tunic, Maz stepped closer, observing the guards and desperately hoping their attention would not shift to them. Both men had a large tattoo of a crescent moon and skull on the side of their necks, which didn't exactly speak a friendly greeting. She dragged Hap a few more steps, and just as it seemed safe to pass through, metal struck metal.

CLANG!

Maz flinched back and then reopened her eyes to find crossed blades at her face. Beyond that was the attention of the hostile, savage eyes.

"What are these hairless things doing here?" one of the guards asked in a scratchy, vicious tone.

"What shall we do to them, Gakit?" asked the other. He used his slouched shoulder to wipe away a pendulum of drool, before turning his rotting smile to await the answer.

"They're from a dome," Mitch answered, returning to intervene. "They're here to help with the war against the Ants."

Maz wanted to challenge that statement, but Gakit's cold stare kept her silent.

"They don't look much use," he said. He moved his tall blade to allow them entry and shifted his eyes back to Logan. Tamak copied, snorting with amusement as Maz darted through, dragging Hap behind her.

"We're not fighting Ants," Maz whispered angrily to Mitch.

"Shh," he whispered back. "You're not going to–"

He was interrupted by Logan's saddened voice, causing them to turn.

"Mitch, my friend."

The guards sniggered, with their blades crossed against Logan's neck like giant scissors. There was a scraping sound as they forced his smiling head back. "Why are we waiting?" asked Gakit. "Let's start the war against the Ants right now!"

Mitch's breathing became audible, and he stomped back to the guards, pointing a stiff finger at his robot companion. "I haven't got time for this, let him through!" he yelled. "Or I'll tell Krakat what you said."

The guards ignored him for a moment, snarling at the unwelcome guest, but then Gakit turned a confused face. "What did we say?" he asked.

"I heard you," Mitch snapped back. "You said the chieftain is a feeble warrior and shouldn't be your leader."

"I didn't say that," Gakit growled.

Mitch spread his arms. "We all heard you," he said. "And Krakat hardly needs persuasion when it comes to slaying challengers, does he?"

Gakit didn't answer. He had the face of someone recalling traumatic memories. Tamak didn't appear too comfortable either.

"Move your damned spears!"

The blades withdrew, and with a forgiving smile, Logan trudged past the guards to rejoin his friends.

The two small crackling fires caused Maz to break a sweat, and the idea of changing the Skullkrakat culture now escaped from her head in the form of beads of liquid, running down her neck. Her first impression of these horrid savages suggested they were better not lured to the surface after all.

She followed Mitch to a nearby wall, where he swept aside a tall sheet of poorly illustrated textile to reveal a dirty entrance: a door-shaped hole smashed through the passage. Maz held the material to one side as she stepped through behind him, and she found herself in a larger chamber, dug into the ground and illuminated by a flaming torch in each corner. A big banner was spread across the opposite wall, displaying a crescent moon and skull symbol, a bigger version of the neck tattoo.

"We're here," Mitch said. He waited a moment as Hap stumbled in and leaned against the mud wall. Logan then raised his bowed head as he thumped through last.

Mitch gestured to one side, where an arch of stone blocks framed an entrance to a descending passage. "The old village," he said. He then pointed to an opening on the other side, the most carelessly dug so far. "The new village," he said, and choosing that direction, he stepped into the tall burrow marked with famished flowers, sagging out of crude, broken pottery.

Maz was nervous about meeting more of the Skullkrakat. For a moment, she considered turning back, but that would involve passing the guards without Mitch to protect her. It was too late; she had no choice but to trust him.

"Come on, friends," said Logan.

Maz waved Hap to follow, and she entered the crude passage, which began to spiral upwards as she pursued her guide. She was soon struggling, but despite her burning leg muscles and shortness of breath, she persisted towards the faint, bitter aroma of leaves that rushed at her face, inviting her to the intensifying, welcome daylight of the surface.

Just inside the end of the tunnel, Mitch stood leaning on the wall with the most casual of poses imaginable, like he'd been waiting for ages. His shallow breaths seemed a struggle, and then an accidental gasp for more oxygen gave him away. He turned quickly and stepped outside, causing an eruption of young, excited voices.

"Mitch, Mitch!"

Maz shielded her eyes from the attacking sunlight as her feet met with the dry and dusty ground, home to a few small islands of short bunched grass with tiny yellow flowers peeking out. In the broader clearing, villagers lounged around on a scattering of wooden benches and stools, enjoying a pleasant conversation. Most appeared to be young adults: broad-shouldered men with long hair and women who were taller. Several stilted huts surrounded the social area, and a high fence separated the village from the dense forest beyond.

Hap collapsed on a Hap-sized patch of grass. Maz wasn't surprised; it looked invitingly soft and spongy, and he'd been craving this moment for some time. She felt exposed and nervous where she stood, with her white clothes and bald head, and it wasn't long before the children bothering Mitch began to notice her, fixing their gawping faces on her one at a time.

The tallest girl approached first. "Where's your hair?" she asked.

Maz opened her mouth to answer but closed it again. It was a stupid question; it wasn't anywhere. She looked at Mitch, expecting him to intervene, but he smirked at her obvious discomfort behind a clenched fist.

"Are you from a dome?" a sweet voice asked as the swarm of staring faces engulfed her.

Maz wanted to poke all the eyes to get rid of them, but instead, she nodded, triggering a chorus of gasps.

Villagers elsewhere started to turn from their conversations, whispering, with curious eyes and wry smiles.

"Mitch is from a dome, and *he* has hair," the taller girl pointed out.

Mitch is from a dome? Maz thought.

"Right, that's enough!" Mitch yelled, and he began shooing them away.

"Little cretins," he said. "Spoilt another surprise, didn't they."

"How many?" Maz asked.

Mitch grinned and didn't answer.

"How many domes are there?" Maz asked again, but a nearby pattering sound distracted them. They turned to see a small boy urinating against Logan's leg. The robot was oblivious, of course, smiling as always.

Mitch growled and lunged at the boy, but he was quick to react, scurrying away to absorb the praise of his chuckling, cheering friends.

"There are a few," he answered, with enraged eyes on the child. He turned back to Maz. "I'm your neighbour, and the citizens of my dome are in danger. That's why I need your help."

"I don't understand," said Maz. "What do you want *us* to do?"

Mitch was about to answer the question when a woman of staggering beauty came rushing across the village to greet him.

"Mitch, my love ... you're back at last!" She flung her arms around him as they collided, and then planted kisses all over his screwed-up face. It was a blatant act of intimacy, which was forbidden back in the dome. It gave Maz a weird feeling as she watched them.

"So, you found some strange-looking hairless people," the woman said, noticing Maz and the collapsed heap on the ground. She was taller than Mitch and had the neck tattoo, but she didn't seem as hostile as the guards until she turned a hateful glance at Logan.

Mitch introduced her as Sanbon, the daughter of Krakat. As the only surviving child of the chieftain, she would one day inherit leadership, if unchallenged.

"Welcome to our village," she said to Maz with a warm smile. "You are witnessing the beginning of something great. The people you see here are the bravest, those willing to embrace change. With the knowledge Mitch brings us from the domes, we can rebuild human civilisation together and reclaim the planet." She hugged a strong arm around Mitch, who looked very pleased with himself.

"Have a rest here," Mitch said to Maz. "Hap may be down a while, and we've got things to catch up on." He turned to Sanbon, and they smiled longingly at one another. He then took her hand and led her back to the tunnel.

Hap's twitching arm indicated he was still alive as Maz selected a patch of grass near to his. She lay back, and it was thick and spongy, as luxurious as she'd imagined. Her closed eyelids glowed orange under the bright sun, which warmed her face and melted her fatigued body into the ground. She ignored the thought of watchful eyes and dreamed of being on the grass near the old wise one, in the safety of her garden back home.

Chapter 7

Maz sat up suddenly, coated with sweat and with a mouth as dry as the dusty ground around her. The heat from the sun no longer comforted her, and she longed for the coolness of the shade and liquid refreshment of some kind. She pushed herself up from the grass cushion and adjusted her twisted tunic. "Hap, wake up," she said. She shook her friend with a dirty foot. Logan had disappeared without making a sound, or she may have been absent in illegal sleep, she wasn't quite sure. "Hap, let's go," she said. "We need liquid." She kicked him harder until he groaned and started rubbing at his eyes.

"I need liquid," he said.

"That's what I just said!"

He casually rose to his feet, but then his whole body trembled, and he staggered forward.

"What are you doing?" Maz asked.

"I think I need to reboot."

"No, you don't. Mitch must have quit reboot. It's about time he answered our questions."

A small group of villagers across the clearing turned to them and smiled; a woman raised a hesitant wave.

"We need to get out of here," Maz whispered, "before anyone tries talking to us."

The woman shared words with her friends, who nodded in response. They then started walking over.

"Oh, no. People are coming. Quick!" She grabbed Hap's arm, and they fled into the spiral tunnel. "Go, go, go!" she said, pushing him forward.

"I'm going, I'm going," he complained as he ran ahead of her.

"Go faster then!" Her feet were clipping his heels.

The end arrived much sooner than expected and with a struggle to slow down, Maz stamped into the entrance room, tripped over Hap, and they landed in a crumpled heap on the floor.

Maz rolled off her friend, clutching her nose, and lowered her face to her knees, wincing until the throbbing agony began to subside. She wiped her watery eyes with the collar of her tunic, but a snorting laugh then startled her. The powerful figures of Gakit and Tamak towered over them, but the guards were not alone. Behind them, another figure stood, with a thick scar dividing his grey beard. The still darkness of his eyes sent a shiver down the metal fixings on Maz's spine.

Gakit snarled down, but this time he didn't speak.

"What shall we do to them, Krakat?" Tamak asked.

The chieftain observed in silence, as though searching his mind for unimaginable evil. Maz closed her eyes to escape him, but then, to her relief, Mitch and Sanbon's voices rose from the old village tunnel.

"I don't like it when he watches us, Mitch. You should take him back to wherever you found him."

"He's not going anywhere. He's just learning about being a person."

The couple emerged at the stone arch, with Logan smiling behind them.

"How would you like it if Tamak watched us?" Sanbon asked, pointing at the guard.

"Watched what?" Tamak asked.

Mitch stepped into the room, glancing cautiously at Krakat, and then confronted the guards. "Gakit, Tamak, step away," he ordered. "They are no concern of yours."

"No concern?" Gakit said with a dry laugh. "They just dared to attack the chieftain."

"Really," said Mitch, moving his hands to his hips. "And he needs your protection against these terrifying beasts, does he?"

The brute hesitated. "No," he answered softly.

"Weaker than them, is he?" Mitch asked.

Tamak looked nervous.

"Krakat is weaker than no man or beast," Gakit answered. He glanced at his leader and then left for the outer tunnels, grunting as he swiped aside the hanging curtain.

As Tamak followed, the chieftain turned his attention to Logan. He moved his hand to the hilt of his large, curved sword, and revealed his teeth.

Seeing this, Mitch beckoned his followers to hurry. "Come on, let's go. You both need to eat something."

Maz and Hap hurried through the stone arch, and Mitch led the group, hastily, through more flame-lit passages and past more curious stares, until they reached a stone-framed water source, built into a wall.

Maz had tasted death by the time Mitch finished filling a hefty container in front of her. He passed it to Logan, and then Maz took her turn and feasted on the cold water until her stomach strained to explode. She wiped her mouth dry, and after Hap had slurped his fill, they wandered into some smaller tunnels and rooms, which Sanbon introduced as being their private residence.

"Come on in!" Mitch yelled.

Maz entered what appeared to be the living area, where Mitch stepped around a sculpted block of earth and sat on a tree trunk stool the other side. He started laying out sheets of illustrated material and beckoned them to join him.

In a manner that suggested he was trained to do so, Logan stomped to the furthest corner of the room, thumped down the container, and then turned to face inward, holding that position. Near to him, the rear wall had been dug into, creating a work surface, home to a variety of unfamiliar items. Sanbon stood at the other end with her back turned, busy with something.

Maz took a stool opposite Mitch, and Hap sat beside her. The wood was hard and uncomfortable compared to the grass, but she rested her elbows on her knees and watched Mitch as he fumbled and flipped his sheets. She couldn't quite make sense of the words or drawings, but she assumed it was all related to his mission. He swept them aside as Sanbon delivered a large wooden tray to the table.

"You won't get your normal nutrients here," she said to them, sitting down beside Mitch with a bright smile. "But I've prepared a traditional Skullkrakat meal for you."

"What's this?" Hap asked, pointing at an orange semi-circle with a fascinating pattern.

"Orange. It grows on the surface," Sanbon answered.

"I can see it's orange," said Hap, "but what is it?"

"Orange," Sanbon repeated.

"I can see that, but–"

"I think the food is named orange, Hap," Maz interrupted.

Sanbon turned a smile to Mitch, but he gazed away, shaking his head.

"Ah!" Hap said with a nod. "So, these are browns then."

"That's meat, you idiot!" Mitch snapped. He reached forward and grabbed a handful of the small chunks.

"Oh right," Hap said with a smirk, obviously revitalised after his illegal sleep. "Well, it's nice to *meat* you guys." He popped a piece in his mouth and then turned to Maz for approval.

"Ha, ha, ha!" Logan boomed from the corner.

"It's not funny, Logan," Mitch said.

"But according to my calculations it is funny, Mitch, my friend," the robot responded. "Hap made a statement which directed my thought process to a primary meaning, but I reacted to indicate that I also identified the secondary meaning."

Sanbon sighed, which seemed to create tension in the room. Mitch chewed on his meat so aggressively that Maz could hear every chomp. She took a few pieces herself and chewed for so long it caused her jaw to ache. After forcing it down, she selected a slice of orange, with its fascinating pattern and texture. She placed it in her mouth, but the moment it touched her tongue, she screwed up her face, and it dropped to the ground.

"Sorry," she said, sucking away the weird, sharp sensation.

Hap chuckled, but then his body twitched a few times; his movement briefly took Mitch's attention away from the floor.

"I hope it doesn't get worse," Maz said, hoping to provoke an explanation.

"Me too," said Hap.

"I wonder why it's happening?" Maz watched Mitch as she spoke.

He raised his head a little, now chewing in a calmer manner. "Chemical withdrawal," he said, moving his mouthful aside so his voice could pass. "Obedience through addiction. He'll be fine soon."

"Reboot?" Maz asked.

Mitch swallowed his meat. "Yes, reboot," he answered clearly.

"But why am I different?" Maz asked. "Why doesn't it happen to me?"

"It *does* happen to you. You just hide it."

"I don't hide it!"

Mitch seemed to enter troubled thought.

"I'm not like Hap or the others," Maz insisted. "Bel says I'm special because only I use lotion."

"What?" Mitch said abruptly. His tone was angry, but his face surprised. Sanbon placed a hand on his leg and whispered to calm him.

"Lotion. It arrives with my nutrients."

"You're lying," he said. He slapped his hands on his thighs and stood to his feet. He moved towards the door, rubbing his forehead and turned. "It's getting late," he said, "but there's something else we want to show you."

◊

As daylight started to fade, Maz was crunching through leaves and twigs again as Mitch led them up a steep hill outside the new village. She considered whether one of his secrets could be untiring robotic legs, hidden beneath his trousers.

"How dark does it get at night?" she asked.

"Sometimes you can't see anything," Sanbon answered.

A lamp swinging and clunking at Mitch's belt, ready to be awoken, eased this concern.

"And Ants?" Maz asked.

"Not at night, don't worry." Sanbon gave her a reassuring smile. The confidence in her stride suggested many nights spent hunting outside, and the large, curved sword at her waist offered protection.

They stepped into a clearing at the top of the hill, and Maz gasped in astonishment at the vast spectacle that filled her view.

"It's called a sunset," said Mitch. "Amazing, isn't it?"

She admired the rippling glow of colours which spanned the horizon, in patterns of wavy, textured cloud; this alone was worth all the walking today. "It's more beautiful than a master creators visual design project," she said.

Mitch and Sanbon took a seat on the grass in front of her, and Logan lowered himself in a bunglesome manner nearby.

Hap brushed against Maz's leg as he settled close, which triggered an unusual emotion, like when she'd witnessed intimacy earlier that day. She sat down and allowed her arm to rest against his; he was warm, silent and motionless, watching the sunset, which reflected in his wide eyes. He looked so much better without a beard, but as she tried to imagine him with hair like Mitch, something beyond him caught her eye. "Domes!" she cried.

She hugged Hap's arm to pull him closer and directed his attention to the landscape beside them. The forest stretched as far as she could see, but scattered throughout it were domes, more than she could count. She marvelled at the idea that each one must contain a dome leader, strange folk, and even a garden like hers.

Mitch pointed out their home and the route walked that day. Behind them was the dome from which he'd escaped, and in the far distance, nestled between two areas of mountainous terrain, stood the remains of a huge, concrete wall marking the restricted area from where the spacecraft once launched.

Maz was awestruck, but soon the last of the colour left the sky and the view faded. With the temperature dropping, she hugged Hap for warmth, resting her head on his shoulder, like Mitch was doing to Sanbon. He was as rigid as an Ash-bot, thumping to the beat of his heart, which was therapeutic, but then, without warning, Mitch fired up his lamp and she released her grasp.

Mitch laughed. "The dome's eyes cannot see you here," he said as he returned to his feet. "Come on. We need a good night's sleep. Tomorrow we begin your part of the mission."

Chapter 8

What the–

Maz awoke to a light pressure across her chest. She opened her eyes and used her thumb and forefinger to relocate Hap's intruding arm. Beside her ear, his mouth gaped open, emitting a soft, creaking sound from his throat.

She lifted the thin sheet of fabric from her body and rolled away, almost knocking over a cup of water which she gladly gulped down. A tiny flame at the wall illuminated the small room, creating just enough light to reveal nothing more than two cups and some rumpled bedding, tangled across her sleeping friend. Her legs ached from the previous day's toil as she stood from the cold, smooth-trodden earth and straightened her tunic. She poked Hap's ribs with her big toe, and he snorted. "Get up," she said.

Being underground, Maz had no idea whether night had turned to day, or for how long illegal sleep should last, but she was alert and awake, proving she didn't need reboot. "Get up," she said again, louder this time, with a harder kick.

Hap groaned and lifted his head. "Why?" he grumbled, squinting at her in the faint orange glow.

"It's morning," Maz answered, and a smile grew on her face. "Today is our mission. Let's go and find Mitch."

Hap moved the sheet lazily to one side and rose reluctantly to his feet. Maz parted the textile curtain at the doorway, stepped out to the passage, and hurried to the living area, hoping her hosts were awake. She poked her head inside.

"Come in!" Mitch shouted to his guests, in a tone more suited to the opposite. He sat on the same stool, perusing his sheets of scribbled material. Logan smiled from his corner, and Sanbon clattered around at the back wall.

As Maz sat down, Sanbon turned with a quiet sniff and delivered another tray of meat and orange to the table. "Did you have a nice sleep?" she asked, with a slight quiver in her voice. Her forced smile was made evident by her puffy, glistening eyes.

"Excuse us a minute," Mitch said before they could answer.

He stood and left the room, and Sanbon followed at a slower pace, wiping her eyes with the back of her hand.

Maz tried to ignore the loud conversation in the next passage by returning her aching jaw and brave taste buds to the problematic pieces on the tray.

"But what if I *were* to bear your child, Mitch?"

"I've told you before. The dome must have damaged my seed. How many times must I tell you this?"

"But what if you're wrong? Do you think I'd allow an Ant anywhere near my new-born?"

"He's not a damned Ant! He's my best friend, and he's staying. And I'm not wrong, so drop it!"

Moments later, Mitch returned alone.

"I'm sorry, Mitch, my friend," said Logan from the corner.

"Just shut up and pour our guests a drink."

Mitch retrieved three small cups from the back wall and slammed them on the table as he sat back down. He swept his hair back and sighed.

Logan galumphed over wielding a large steaming jug. He leaned down and poured a dark liquid into the cups, and Mitch pushed one across the table to each of his guests, almost spilling them.

"Coffee," he said. "It's a primitive form of reboot, a popular drink in the old world. We now grow the plants near the new village."

With yearning eyes, Hap moved a shaky hand towards the cup, but on contact, he gasped and flinched back. "It hurt my hand," he said.

Mitch shook his head and whispered "Idiot" into his shoulder. "The liquid is hot," he said. "Like the fires in the tunnels? Like the sun that blurred your eyes? It's the traditional old-world way."

With the cup remaining on the table, Maz held it for as long as she could before the pain became unbearable. Hap did the same, and then they grabbed at the same time, grinning in agonising competition. A cough from Mitch soon halted the contest.

Hap tasted the drink, but then peered into the cup and returned it to the table.

"Can you tell us what our mission is now?" Maz asked.

Mitch sipped his coffee and then cleared his throat. "Yes," he said. "You've learnt the secrets of the outside, so today you learn the secrets of the inside."

"Inside the dome?" Maz asked.

"That's right," he answered. "But you might not like what you find."

"What do you mean?"

He took another swig. "Today you will see what the domes are capable of. My people have become prisoners, locked away to meet a slow demise. My dome leader has collapsed into insanity, so I need you to witness the truth and persuade your leader to help me instead.” Maz nodded as he spoke. “I *must* save them and deliver them to a life of freedom with the Skullkrakat. They will work to expand the new village; then, as the borders grow, I will enter more domes, rescuing them from enslavement. And one day soon, a city will stand here once more, from where the future success of humankind can be born." He gazed into his mind, with full and certain eyes.

Maz raised her hot coffee to her lips, and a strong, unpleasant aroma hit her nostrils. She took a tiny sip, and a bitterness attacked her tongue, so she quickly swallowed and returned the cup to the table. "Bel will help, I'm sure of it," she said. "We can go and speak to her. What do you need us to say?"

"No, not yet," Mitch said. "I need you to witness the danger we face. Otherwise, you'll be back in your pod the moment you return."

"No, I won't," said Maz. "I'm different."

"You keep saying you're different, that you're special," said Mitch, "but you're not. *I'm* the saviour of human civilisation, not you. I revealed secrets to you, and now you pay for them. It's not too late for me to feed you to the Ants."

He took a deep breath to calm down and then made an expression like he'd forgotten something. Then he remembered: "So I'm taking you to my dome," he said, and he gulped down the last of his coffee.

"Are you going there, Maz?" Hap asked in a shaky voice.

"Well, yes," she answered. "If that's the plan."

"Okay."

Mitch unfolded one of his sheets of material on the table and prodded the surface. "It's not far," he said. He slid his finger back and forth along dotted lines, which ran between a small dome shape and a skull inside a sun – a symbol similar to that of the Skullkrakat. Maz guessed the long rectangles were mounds.

"You seem well rested," he said. "We'll set off soon." He screwed up the map and launched it across the table at Maz, who caught the unravelling sheet and stuffed it in her tunic pocket. "In case we get split up again," he added. "Now go and find Sanbon in the armoury. She's been keen to show you the array of weapons. I'll meet you there shortly."

Maz remembered that on the previous day they had passed an entrance near the residence which Sanbon had introduced with enthusiasm as the armoury. The weapons framing the door were what Mitch had referred to as 'spears', although the bladed sections were even more massive than Sanbon's sword, spanning half of the thick wooden stem. It hardly seemed the safest place to start the day, but Maz was keen to get moving, so she and Hap stood and left the room.

Mitch leaned across the table to collect the cups. *What a waste*, he thought. He put his thumb into one and then used his fingers to clamp them all together as he grabbed the jug with his other hand. He stepped to the back wall and then gulped down what his guests had wasted before dropping the cups into a pot of water. He retrieved a small cloth and splashed them around, giving them a good clean.

At last, he had contact with another dome, and now the mission could progress. This was his purpose, so he was wrong to have experienced any doubt as he waited for many days in the darkness beneath the tree, listening for human voices, scared to venture deeper into the danger of another dome. The burrows took a long time to dig, even with the help of Sanbon's strong arms, so his worst fear was finding it empty, or already filled with corpses. But that would never happen; he was never destined to fail.

As he lifted the last cup from the water and shook it dry, he sensed a movement behind him. He turned around, and it slipped from his grasp, thudding to the earth beneath his feet.

"Krakat," he said, through a rush of nerves.

The chieftain watched him, motionless and silent.

Mitch laughed nervously. "Would you like some meat?" he asked, gesturing at the table between them. He turned to Logan who stood smiling at the visitor from the corner. He felt safer with his robot companion but wished he could modify the facial expression to achieve a more fearsome deterrent.

"Or maybe some orange?" he asked, but Krakat didn't answer.

Mitch looked around the room, for nothing in particular, and laughed again as the chieftain's hand moved to the hilt of his sword.

"You will cease relations with my daughter," Krakat ordered, in a heavy, authoritative tone. The force of the commanding voice pushed Mitch back against the work surface.

"Um, I think you're being a little hasty there, Krakat."

"You will cease relations with my daughter," the chieftain said again.

Mitch was terrified of Krakat, but soon he and the other ageing warriors would rot underneath the new world. With Sanbon as his queen, Mitch would rule the surface, and nobody could ruin that dream. "My apologies, Krakat," he said. "I didn't mean to make her cry."

The chieftain unsheathed his massive, shimmering blade and aimed it down his cold stare. He began circling the table.

Mitch was trapped. He hurried over to Logan in the corner and nestled beside him, attempting to hide behind the strong frame. He peered around the robot's broad shoulder to see Krakat moving closer, staring down his blade. "Do something, Logan," he whispered.

Logan turned his smiling face. "There's a low probability of success from a physical response, Mitch, my friend. And I believe you are more equipped for a verbal response."

"I don't care, just do something," Mitch whispered, trembling as the point of the blade squashed against the tip of his nose.

"Leave my friend alone!" Logan shouted, turning his smiling face to Krakat and breaking his stare. He then waved his arms and ploughed forward, causing the chieftain to stumble back and collapse near the table, dropping his sword.

Krakat scrambled to his feet with a burst of aggressive energy and the face of a thunderstorm and flexed every rippling muscle as he clawed his fingers and roared at the ceiling, shaking the atmosphere of the room.

Mitch edged along the wall in the direction of the door. He didn't fancy being on the receiving end of such a mighty destructive power. His tunnel life was now over.

Logan was smiling and unprepared when Krakat leapt forward and wrapped his bulging arms around him, wrestling him down. He slammed the robot's head on Mitch's stool with an incredible force. *DONK!* And the smashing repeated, to the song of deep, diabolical laughter. *DONK! DONK! ... DONK! ... DONK!*

He clenched a beastly arm around Logan's neck, and the other around his leg, and with seemingly superhuman strength and biceps bursting, he hoisted the robot to head-height and slammed him down on the table. *CLUMP!* He then lifted the flailing body again and repeated this action numerous times, as his grey beard danced to the rumble of his laughter. *CLUMP! ...CLUMP! ... CLUMP!*

Mitch edged along the wall a little further, trying to slip away unnoticed, as Krakat stamped his foot down on Logan's body, forcing him off the table and into a heap among the stools, covered in mashed up meat and orange.

"Pathetic," he spat as he retrieved his sword.

Mitch froze still. It was too late to escape. He would have to rely on superior intelligence, otherwise, suffer the same fate. "Does Sanbon not have a choice?" he asked.

Krakat sheathed his blade. "She has a choice," he answered. "As long as the man has seed, so my bloodline does not die with her."

He heard the argument. Mitch panicked for excuses, but he couldn't deny his own spoken words. "I have seed," he lied. "It's just the stress of trying to save–"

"Listen to me, Mitch, and listen strong," Krakat growled. "You will cease relations with my daughter, and if you dare challenge me, or speak of this to her – or anyone, I will crush you like I have your feeble Ant."

Lacking a response, Mitch marched out of the room while the chieftain's sword remained sheathed. He rushed down the next passage and swiped the curtain to his sleeping quarters aside as he entered. Heavy footsteps passed outside, and he considered murdering the beast, but he was not tough enough to do it himself, and the Skullkrakat were a loyal tribe. If the chieftain had enemies, they would never live long enough to make it known, so there was little or no chance of recruiting a stronger man.

He tore off his black clothes, dumped them on the floor, and rummaged around in a storage space in the wall. He threw out more black garments until he found a white tunic which he slung over his head.

Logan stumbled in, smiling as always, but with a badly dented head. "I'm sorry, Mitch, my friend," he said, sadly.

Mitch stormed over to him and ripped off his shirt. "Useless robot," he muttered. He struggled to remove the trousers, mumbling and growling to himself, yanking them hard. "Stay still!" he complained. "No! Apart from that leg. Lift that leg!"

Without access to a large white tunic, Logan was left looking no different to a damned Ant, which further infuriated Mitch, causing him to lash at the wall repeatedly with the abandoned Skullkrakat outfit. He moved the curtain aside, peered into the passage, then set off in a furious march towards the armoury.

"Come on, you idiots, we're leaving!" he yelled as he arrived.

The room glistened like a sacred space as hundreds of heavy, serrated blades reflected the light of small flames. A curved dagger rested on Sanbon's palm, the smallest of the weapons being forged, but one of her favourites. The bald heads had been leaning in, listening intently, but the presentation was now over.

"I said, come on!" Mitch yelled. He then turned to escape the beautiful eyes of the woman he loved. It was time to leave the tunnels, never to return.

Chapter 9

Back in the outer tunnels, the group headed in a new direction towards Mitch's dome. In a tunic instead of shirt and trousers, he looked like a young dome leader with his hair. Logan plodded along unclothed, like an Ant, but with severe damage to his head. He smiled as always and was only a robot after all, but the further they walked, the more Maz became curious, yet she lacked enough bravery to interrupt the aggressive march of her guide.

After a long walk on already sore leg muscles, a glow of natural light revealed steps up ahead. Maz squinted her aching eyes as they readjusted to the daylight outside and she found herself in the forest once again, with a dome wall ahead of her, a short distance through the trees. Mitch led them to another camouflaged hatch, which he flipped up to reveal a burrow. Maz then remembered the treacherous crossing and turned to Hap to find his face now whiter than his tunic. He nodded at Maz, or he bounced his head to encourage himself; she couldn't tell which. He gazed at the hole and swallowed back his twitching frown.

Mitch glanced in every direction and delivered his instructions: "Logan," he said, turning to his damaged companion. "Wait here as normal. But remember, if you see any Ants you must lead them away from the hatch *and* the tunnel entrance. Alright?"

"Yes, Mitch, my friend."

He then turned to the others. "You both follow me. The layout should be the same. You'll witness the peril, and then we escape fast. Got it?"

Maz nodded.

"We avoid Ashers at all cost. Got it?" he added. He then scrambled into the burrow.

"Got it," Maz answered.

Hap turned to her, looking worried. "Are you sure this is safe?" he asked.

"And close the hatch behind you!" yelled a muffled voice from below.

"I'm sure it's fine," Maz answered. She knelt to the ground and entered the darkness.

The hatch thumped closed, and Mitch's lamp ignited to reveal the space up ahead. Maz scrambled from the burrow and then the sight of the vast gridded black pit made her queasy. *It's just walking in a straight line. Easy,* she thought. But it wasn't, and neither was pulling herself up through the hole in the mesh, even with Mitch giving her a bunk-up. Her searching fingers soon tapped on wood, and she lifted the hatch, revealing the beautiful sight of a lush green lawn.

"Check for Ashers!" Mitch whispered from behind.

Maz crawled out, holding the hatch for Hap until his hand emerged. She stood and ran her fingertips across the craggy, familiar skin of the ancient tree, and while resting the flat of her hands against the rough surface, she sidestepped over a root collar and leaned out to check the space ahead. The garden appeared to be the same as back home; even the flowers and shrubs were growing in the same positions. "It's clear," she said.

"Good," Mitch answered, slapping dirt from his tunic as he stood. "Let's get moving."

They hurried across the grass towards the gateway and reached the soft, grey surface of the terrace. The familiar and comfortable sensation beneath Maz's feet caused a brief release of tension throughout her body.

"Wait here," Mitch said, pointing to the bench from where their adventure began. He sneaked through the gateway and into the Outer Zone corridor.

They took a seat, and Maz turned to where the Ash-bot had been snipping at the shrub on the previous day. She imagined for a moment that the dome had rewound time, giving her a chance to denounce her suspicions and stop meddling in betrayal. She had no doubt that life had been safe, secure and certain so far, but she longed for something more, and a recovered planet waited for her, with a big plan to retake it. She couldn't allow herself to be imprisoned in her pod while the new world emerged without her.

"Come on. It's clear!" Mitch shouted from the gateway.

Maz stood. *I've made my choice*, she thought, and with Hap by her side, she followed Mitch into the Outer Zone.

Each corridor and junction matched those of back home, as Mitch had suggested, and the north block soon appeared in front of them. Maz entered the town circle, but some differences caught her eye; a dark grey material covered most of the rooms, preventing her from seeing the pod's inside, and beyond the south block opposite stood a taller, more sinister structure, growing from the Outer Zone and clasping the dome ceiling. No strange folk lurked, but Maz wanted to leave as soon as possible; Mitch's dome seemed familiar, yet shrouded in strong, negative energy which weighed in the atmosphere.

"Why are the rooms covered?" Hap asked, pointing up.

"So you can't see the prisoners clawing at the front of their cells as they slowly perish," Mitch answered.

Maz imagined them sitting on the floor behind each surface, pleading for help and scratching to escape. "How do we get them out?" she asked.

"That's a question for your leader," Mitch answered. "I need you to ask for security override codes and details of hidden exits or vulnerabilities for evacuation. You need to make her realise that her dome could be next, so we need to fight back now."

"Bel will help us," said Maz.

"Good," said Mitch. "But make sure you get her alone, you can't–" He turned his head. "Shh," he whispered, and he listened. "Move. Now!"

They rushed to the side of the gateway, into the edge of the Vegetation Zone, and rested their backs against the dark green wall. Mitch peered his head back into the corridor as clattering and scrambling sounds arose from inside. "We'll need to hide behind the plants," he said.

Maz stepped towards the greenery, but a sound stopped her in her tracks. *SNIP ... SNIP-SNIP ... SNIP*. She reversed her steps as the side of a head emerged from among the plants, partly transparent with a visible circuit-board. The Ash-bot focused on the stems and leaves, not the humans, yet they were trapped, nonetheless. *SNIP-SNIP ... SNIP*. They returned their backs to the wall and Mitch peered into the corridor again, where the sound had drawn much closer.

"Asher scum!" a man's voice shouted.

Mitch held Maz by the tunic and guided her until they switched positions. He whispered for her to witness, and her heart raced. Inside the corridor, eight Ash-bots wrestled an angry man towards an unmarked doorway; two robots gripped each limb as he struggled and kicked at his captors, refusing to get dragged into the room. The man managed to free an arm and grabbed the door-frame, but the Ash-bots overpowered him, and the sliding door soon whooshed closed, leaving behind silence. Maz crept into the corridor, and Mitch and Hap followed.

"Can we leave now?" Hap asked, looking terrified.

Mitch glanced outside to check the other Ash-bot wasn't following. He returned to them, nodding. "I think you've seen enough," he said.

Maz agreed. She was scared and must warn Bel of the danger.

Halfway back to the garden, Mitch took an unexpected turn down a side passage. He stepped up to a door and glanced both ways. *NOK ... NOK-NOK ... NOK-NOK-NOK*. They waited a moment, and after a light clunk, the sliding door whooshed open. On the other side stood a grinning child with messy black hair, swinging an Ash-bot arm back and forth as though it were a toy.

"Ah, chosen one. How can I be of service?" the boy asked.

"What have you found?" Mitch asked him, impatiently.

The boy turned to Maz and Hap and chuckled at them.

"What have the disciples reported?" Mitch asked. "Tell me!"

"You don't have many left, chosen one," the boy answered. "Been taken away like the rest of 'em."

Mitch moved to the opposite wall. He took a deep breath and rubbed his face hard with both hands.

The boy pointed the Ash-bot arm at Maz and Hap. "How many segments clean are they?" he asked.

Mitch stomped back to the doorway, grabbed the boy's tunic, and shook him for answers. "You must have found something?" he asked with an enraged face.

"Get off me, chosen one," the boy complained. He wriggled free and swung the Ash-bot arm, whacking Mitch on the thigh. "I've been searching in the south, found some new areas, you *idiot*."

Mitch winced, rubbing his leg. He shook his head like he was resisting retaliation. "And?!" he said. "Is that all you can report since last time?"

The boy smirked at him, but then a garbled song from the main corridor caught everyone's attention.

Mitch bundled everyone into the doorway. "Close it, quick," he said.

The sound grew louder, in tones of gibberish, broken at times by a spluttering cough. Mitch stepped out to greet Bernard, the damaged dome leader.

"Mitch. Is that you?" the old man mumbled through his bushy white beard.

He took a deep breath as he straightened his back, lifting his nose to create an air of importance. He raised both hands to clutch his silver livery collar and cleared his throat as he approached. "Mitch," he said, stopping in front of him.

"Bernard, you mustn't give up hope."

"Give up hope?" the dome leader replied. He muttered some nonsense and laughed as he brushed Mitch's shoulder and continued walking. "Mustn't give up hope, he says."

The old man walked away. "I could do with your help!" Mitch shouted. Bernard laughed again, this time mockingly, as he turned a corner and disappeared.

For a moment, Mitch considered sneaking back to steal a dagger from the armoury and forcing the crazy man to provide answers. But he would only receive laughter in response, or information leading to further harm. He returned to the door. *NOK ... NOK-NOK ... NOK-NOK-NOK*. It whooshed open, and the boy stepped out with a terrified face.

"The Ashers have taken your friends away, chosen one!"

"Wha–"

Maz pushed the boy aside as she and Hap emerged from the room, and the boy chuckled at Mitch's angry face.

"Search every detail of the south," Mitch spat at him. "The ventilation spaces. Scale the walls. Whatever it takes. I need to know everything."

"Yes, chosen one," the boy replied.

"And don't get caught with that!" Mitch pointed at the Ash-bot arm.

"Yes, chosen one," the boy said again. He leapt through the door, which slid closed behind him.

Mitch turned a red face to his followers. "We're finished here. Let's go."

Chapter 10

After visiting Mitch's dome, the danger was now clear. The next orders from Mitch were to report to Bel, out of the earshot of Ash-bots and other citizens, and then obtain the information that he required.

Back in Maz's garden, after a tiresome wait for an Ash-bot to depart, she and Hap emerged from the tree and hurried back into their deceivingly perfect utopia. As they reached the end of the corridor at the town circle gateway, they slowed their steps as they met an unexpected sound of loud voices coming from the direction of the central courtyard. Maz took the path forward, crept down the side of the north block and peered out to observe the disturbance.

"Bob! Bob! Bob! Bob! Bob!" chanted a group of about seven citizens. The bouncing glow of Bel's hair burst free, and with a beaming smile across her face, she raised a wrapped bundle above her head and floated along the western path. The others followed, not smiling, but with curious eyes on the new arrival. They chanted as though by instruction, and one carried a small stringed instrument, strumming a hideous pattern of vibrations. "Bob! Bob! Bob! Bob!" The group then passed the west block and disappeared into a gateway to the Outer Zone. The atmosphere suddenly became silent.

Maz had never witnessed the arrival of a baby before, but after this experience, she hoped never to again. She stepped out from the building and checked for Hap, but he was nowhere in sight. She rushed along the path to the courtyard, glancing around for her friend, but then an ugly noise sounded from the direction of the printer column. She strode over knowingly and discovered him on the other side, admiring a small, stringed instrument with a Logan-sized smile on his face.

"Put it back," she ordered, reaching to snatch it from him.

Hap stepped away and held the instrument close. "That's not very fair," he said. He swept his fingernails across the strings, causing the most terrible racket.

"Put it back," Maz said again. "We need to speak to Bel before anything bad happens here." She reached out, with a strong urge to smash the annoying object.

Hap backed away. "We can't speak to her yet, can we? She's not alone. Didn't you see?" He coughed to clear his throat, and then attempted to sing: "We left our home." *STRUM STRUM STRUM.* "To help Mitch's dome." *STRUM STRUM STRUM.* "We ate meat and orange." *STRUM STRUM STRUM.* "Erm ..." He paused for thought. "What rhymes with orange?"

Before he could continue, Maz wrestled the instrument from him and threw it back into the hatch. Hap lunged to retrieve it, but after a brief struggle, Maz tore it free and raised it above her head in a threat to wallop him. "We don't have time for this," she said, but then a nearby sound startled them. *BEEP BEEP BEEP.*

The pair jerked around as an Ash-bot wandered in from the eastern path. Its dark eyes stared, and a red light blinked from its head. *BEEP BEEP BEEP.* Maz grabbed Hap by the arm, and they stepped back around the column. A shrub near the courtyard then rustled, and another robot rose from behind the leaves with a blank stare. *BEEP BEEP BEEP.* More began to emerge from the paths, and with an awkward bounce, they approached from all directions, beeping and flashing.

After the last one reached the courtyard, they formed a circle and paused to observe their targets. They bounced a little closer and paused again.

"What do we do?" Hap whispered. "Do they know ... that we know?"

Maz shot a glance between each Ash-bot as she panicked with frantic thoughts. Escaping the dome now would cause Mitch to fail, leaving them vulnerable on the outside, but they couldn't seek Bel's help amongst a keen crowd of citizens, and with Ash-bots pursuing them.

The circle closed in.

"Shall we just run?" Hap whispered. He stepped a foot forward and waited for a movement from Maz.

"It's alright," she answered. "Trust me."

The opportunity passed, and as Maz dodged aside, four Ash-bots lunged at Hap, grappling with his battling limbs. They hoisted him from the ground and carried away his wriggling body. "Maz! Help!" he cried.

Hap was long overdue a reboot, so they should've seen this coming. The threat of Mitch's dome couldn't cloud every judgement, so Maz chose to act normal to protect the secrecy of the mission. As Hap disappeared towards the Outer Zone, however, she desperately hoped she was right.

The remaining Ash-bots retained their distance and didn't move to seize her. Motionless, they watched her, beeping and flashing, as though alerting the dome to her presence. For a moment, she waited for something to happen, and then a tender, concerned voice cried out from the west. "Maz, my dear, what is happening?"

Bel raised her tunic from her hurrying legs as she approached along the western path. "Are you alright, Maz?" she asked, panting for breath as she reached the printer column.

"Danger report," announced one of the Ash-bots, stepping forward. The voice surprised Maz, but the robotic tone and motionless face suggested a stored alert, rather than any human level intelligence.

"Open report," Bel said, looking confused.

"Negativity detected. Intent to commit aggression."

Maz stared down at her grubby feet, trying to conceal her obvious guilt.

"Threat dismissed," Bel said, followed by a long sigh.

The Ash-bots stopped beeping and dispersed, leaving behind a silence which was even more terrifying.

"This is very worrying, Maz," Bel said in a soft, yet earnest tone.

Maz couldn't look her in the eye.

"Your tunic is filthy. Illegal sleep in the garden was it?"

She shook her head at the accusation.

"I'm starting to doubt your potential now, Maz. This is *not* the behaviour of a future dome leader now, *is it*?" Her tone hardened.

Maz wanted to explain everything, but she couldn't swallow down the knot in her throat.

"It's not good enough, Maz."

The corners of her frown started to tremble. She attempted to speak, but only a gasp surfaced.

"Rest and reboot ... *immediately!*"

On that command, Maz ran. She never wished to disappoint her leader, only to help her, to warn her of the danger they faced. As she hurried to the south block with tears flowing down her cheeks, she struggled to understand how, with the best intentions, she had now failed both of her leaders and her best friend.

Chapter 11

Nine segments passed, and Maz's eyes shot open as the reboot chemicals rushed through her veins. "Eject!" she said. She almost slipped with her sudden twist, barely cushioning her fall, then lunged to retrieve her tunic, throwing it over her head. "Menu, select," she said, not even considering her options. The invisible hatch on the wall whooshed open, revealing a tall beaker of thick yellow liquid, tailored to her specific nutritional requirements. She grabbed it, gulped about half, then returned it to the hatch and snatched the pot of lotion from inside. She stopped for a moment and ran a hand gently across her head, finding a slight softness on the skin. She lowered a cupped hand, scooped out the substance, then exchanged it for the beaker and reached into the frothy yellow liquid, rippling her fingers until all the cream had dissolved. After wiping the residue on her tunic, she hurried to the front surface of the room, which was thankfully still transparent.

The descent took far too long, but as Maz drummed her legs impatiently, she counted a lucky zero. She leapt from the platform before it reached the ground, sprinted to the courtyard, and took a sharp right turn to the eastern path.

She hurried around the east block to the north face and peered into Hap's room to find the pod open and no sign of him. The memory of the struggling man returned to her thoughts. Was Hap imprisoned in the Outer Zone somewhere? She took a deep, calming breath. *This isn't Mitch's dome,* she reminded herself. *He'll be in the garden, waiting as usual.* She rushed across the grass to the gateway and sprinted through the corridors, wishing this to be true.

"Hap!" She flew past the empty bench and turned in circles on the grass, scanning the space. "Haa 'ap!" She gasped for more oxygen, and dizziness swept in. *What have I done?* she thought. A figure then stepped out from the tree. "Hap?"

She dropped to her knees, and as she regained her breath, her friend crossed the lawn towards her. He crouched down, wrapped her in his arms, and squeezed her tight against his warm body. "You were right," he whispered in her ear. "I'm fine."

Maz sealed her eyes tightly to lock in the tears, but the wetness broke through as she loosened her grip and looked her friend in the eye. "Did they hurt you?" she asked. The patches of hair were gone, and his face suggested concern.

Hap gazed across the grass. "No. It was weird," he said. "But it's fine."

Maz raised a hand to his cheek, returning his eyes to hers. "Then what's wrong?" she asked.

Hap twisted his body and nodded at the tree. "Guess," he said.

An angry red face materialised in Maz's mind; Mitch had been waiting for them all this time.

"He's going for a sleep in the forest, but demands our presence with Bel at sunrise," Hap said. "But that's not for a while."

"Okay," said Maz. "We'll wait here first. Let's hope she'll listen."

◇

A few segments later, Maz and Hap stood from the grass and began the familiar stroll from the garden to the town circle. They had passed the time discussing recent events – especially the mystery of Logan's dented head. If Mitch was angry at him, he could have sent him away, fixing his disagreement with Sanbon. It didn't make any sense; something wasn't right.

They emerged from the corridor into the open space. Maz followed the path to the nearby north block as usual, while the uncivilised Hap jogged across the grass. He stopped in front of his east block and raised a hand to beckon her over.

Maz counted one citizen on a bench in the south. Not much of a problem, but an unnecessary one; she was now a failure in her leader's eyes. She hopped to the grass, feeling pleasantly naughty, and jogged towards Hap who's shocked face erupted with delight before he hurried off, leading the way.

"Over here!" he yelled as he reached the rear corner of the south block. He beckoned Maz to the Vegetation Zone, the least likely place they would find their leader. She panicked for a moment, concerned the shout may have alerted the citizen, but she was now beside the building and out of view of the benches. Hap waited for her among the tall plants between the south gateways, pointing at the rear wall, where an Ash-bot stood wiping the dark green surface with a yellow cloth.

"What are you doing?" Maz asked.

"Watch."

Maz flinched away as the Ash-bot rotated its head; the memory of Hap's arrest would haunt her forever. The lenses shifted as the robot glanced between them, then Hap stepped forward with unexpected confidence. "Question," he said. "Where is the dome leader?"

"In the mainframe," answered a robotic voice.

Hap nodded to himself with a satisfied smile. "Question," he said again. "Where is the mainframe?"

The Ash-bot raised a stiff arm, directing them along the wall to their right, and then spoke in a robotic tone. "Enter corridor. Second left. Third right. Ascend steps. First left."

"Did you get that, Maz?"

We can talk to them? She stared at the Ash-bot in disbelief.

"Maz?"

"Sorry," she said. "Ask again." Requesting help from the enemy seemed like a stupid idea, but she lacked a better one.

Hap turned to the Ash-bot. "Question. Where is the mainframe?"

The robot raised its arm. "Enter corridor. Second left. Third right. Ascend steps. First left."

"Got it," Maz said. "Enter. Second left. Third right–"

"Ascend steps. First Left." A voice from behind her finished the sentence.

Maz span around; the citizen from the bench stood watching, having responded to Hap's careless invitation. "Go away, strange boy," she said to him.

He regarded her with young eyes, and his profile in Maz's AR vision introduced him as Dev, with a pathetic 4.7 average project rating. "What are you doing?" he asked.

"*Go. Away*," Maz answered in a firm voice. "Come on, Hap."

The weird boy continued watching the Ash-bot as the friends marched in the direction of what was hopefully the mainframe and not a devious trap. They weaved through an assemblage of tall plants, and soon reached the gateway. As they followed the instructions through the south Outer Zone, Hap described a forced reboot in a room full of pods, before the Ash-bots requested his questions for a citizen self-improvement session; this punishment is what gave him the idea.

They ascended the steps, and the first door on the left had the word 'Mainframe' written above it; the Ash-bot spoke the truth.

"Impressive," said Maz.

Hap returned a proud grin and held a fist to the door. *NOK NOK NOK*. They waited. Nothing. *NOK NOK ... NOK NOK*. Still no response.

An access panel lay on the wall beside the door, restricting entry. Maz raised her hand, expecting nothing. *WHOOOSH*.

A green hand-print appeared in place of Maz's palm and faded away as she stared in silence. On previous attempts, she accessed nothing more than rooms of broken, brightly-coloured maintenance tools, damaged plants, and pieces of worn turf. She concluded from this that every other unrestricted room would be equally as disappointing. But this was the mainframe, the most important room in the dome.

She stepped through the door and into a white box, about the size of her residence; it had no pod, only a door on the opposite end, identical to the first. Hap rushed ahead and slammed his hand on the panel, but nothing happened. He turned a sad face.

Maz nudged him aside and raised her palm. *WHOOOSH*.

The next room was more significant than the first. Bel stood in the centre, gasping, with a hand across her chest. Beyond her, a vast screen displayed surveillance of a baby suspended inside a tiny pod; this central display was the largest, almost filling the rear wall, but the other two walls had large screens powered down.

"Sorry," said Maz, stepping further into the room. Her legs became weak as the feeling of guilt returned.

"How on earth did you open that?" Bel asked. She made a gesture in the air, and the screen went blank. "You scared the life out of me." Her puzzled expression focused on the door, and she shook her head with half-closed eyes. "You shouldn't be here," she said.

Maz considered speaking, but an overwhelming urge to flee clouded her thoughts. Hap must have sensed this discomfort, as with bubbling confidence from the day's successes, he announced: "We want to tell you the truth."

The ensuing conversation may have gone better in a blissful courtyard encounter, with new high-scoring projects to boast of, but with the recent crime and behaviour warnings, Hap's truth didn't go down too well.

"Giant ant robots?" Bel cried. "Killer domes? The chosen one?"

Maz winced as negative energy she thought impossible continued to rise from her leader.

"This folly stops now! I don't know what you're trying to achieve here, but you're becoming a danger to my community. I'm summoning the Ash-bots."

"No!" Maz ran and grabbed her leader by both her arms. "Bel, please," she pleaded. "He's telling you the truth, I promise you!"

Bel stared down in horror at the clutching hands. "What has Hap done to you?!"

Maz stepped back, clasped her hands together and begged. "I promise. You *must* believe us." Then she remembered. *The map!* She plunged her hand into her tunic pocket. "The map!" she cried with excitement, kneeling to the floor and unravelling it with shaking hands. "Look! Bel, look!" She stabbed the shapes with her finger. "Dome. Mound. Tunnel. Look!"

Bel gazed down over her silver collar, and her eyes widened. "Who have you shown this to?" she asked.

"Nobody," Maz answered. "Mitch said nobody else could know."

Bel took a deep breath. "Good," she said. "And keep it that way." She squatted, snatched the map, and then stood, pausing for a while in troubled thought. Her hand guarded the confiscated material inside her tunic pocket, always moving.

Maz stood as she waited for Bel's quiet mutterings to rise into spoken words.

"Alright, I'll speak to him," she decided. "But everything *must* return to normal as soon as possible. None of this can affect our peaceful community."

"Thank you," said Maz. "He can't do this without you."

Bel didn't smile.

◇

A purple grey filled the sky as they led their silent leader out of the burrow and into the forest clearing. High pitched frequencies screeched from every distant tree as a thousand tiny creatures cried out for the sun, or else it might not come.

Bel glanced around as she stood. Maz couldn't assess her thoughts as the dim morning light kept the finer details of her expression concealed. Two things were certain though – she was *not* happy, and reentering the dome would be the last time she ever stepped over that perilous grid.

"Friends!" boomed a voice from the forest, and a trudging of heavy footsteps followed.

"Don't be scared," Maz whispered. "It's just a big, stupid robot called Logan. He won't hurt you."

Logan bounded into the clearing with a massive smile across his dented head. "Hello, friends!"

"Hi, Logan," said Maz. "We've got another new friend for you. Meet Bel."

"Hello, Bel," he said to the surprised woman. "Does meeting me make you feel happy?"

She turned to Maz, who nodded to encourage her.

"Yes?" she replied hesitantly.

"Is Mitch awake?"

"No, Maz, my friend," the robot answered. "But he ordered me to wait here and bring you to him." He turned around and stomped back into the forest.

The sky was bright and blue by the time they located him, so he must have put some time and thought into finding a perfect tree for a comfortable rest. He may have started the night with his back against it, but his body now curled in the dirt and leaves, rendering his long search pointless. Still excited from the success of his Ash-bot idea, Hap seemed keen to be the one to rouse him, so he crept forward, grinning back at the others, and then leaned down. "Boo!"

CRACK!

Maz laughed, and Bel let out a yelp of concern as Hap collapsed, clutching his nose. Mitch stood, muttering unknowns and pointing a stiff finger. He spotted Maz and marched over instantly.

"Give me the codes," he growled, ruffled-haired and squinting. He held a hand out to Maz, completely ignoring Bel.

"The codes?" Maz asked as Mitch bounced his hand expectantly. "But you wanted Bel out here first, didn't you?"

Mitch threw up his arms, and his face became redder. "Are you an idiot? What did I say to you in my dome? Security codes, vulnerabilities, potential exits!" He marched back to Hap with a waving fist, as though offering a second helping. "Security codes, vulnerabilities, hidden damned exits. Remember?"

Hap leaned away, still clutching his nose.

Mitch withdrew his fist, rested his hands on his hips and took slow, deep breaths.

Bel turned to Maz. "Is the big Ash-bot from his dome?" she asked.

Oh no, Maz thought, regretting the poor planning.

Mitch must have heard, as he went stamping into the forest, throwing his arms around as though angrily explaining something obvious to an invisible being.

His loyal companion trudged off after him, and Hap returned, holding his nose beneath watery eyes.

"Well ... this is the kind of behaviour that occurs when you avoid reboot," Bel advised, giving him a stern glare.

Maz didn't care for her opinion anymore. She watched as Mitch made a full circle and headed back towards them, with Logan smiling merrily, lumbering behind.

Mitch appeared calmer on his return, stopping in front of them with closed eyes, mouthing a silent countdown until his eyelids shot open. "He is *not* an Asher," he said, and he forced a smile. "Hello, Bel. I'm your neighbour. My people are suffering and are close to death, and I've been waiting for these *idiots* all night." He stopped speaking for a moment to puff away the returning rage. "Could you *please* go inside and find me security override codes and details of potential evacuation points so I can save my people. Thank you." His eyes strained under the weight of his smile.

Bel would never sit back and allow people to suffer, yet for some reason, she hesitated to respond. A finger rose to her lips as she considered the situation. "You've both witnessed this?" Maz and Hap nodded, and another silence passed before she spoke again. "Mitch," she said. "My duty is to maintain a high standard in *this* dome." She pointed at the towering wall behind her. "It is not my duty to give away classified information to strangers on the outside, and it is also forbidden for me to communicate with other domes."

Did she know there were other domes? Maz wondered.

"If your words are true, I hope you find a way to help your people," Bel added, turning away. "But I cannot break the rules, and I don't have what you need." She strolled back to the hatch.

"Murderer!" Mitch shouted. "That's what you are!"

"I'm sorry," she said.

Maz followed her into the burrow, begging her to change her mind.

Chapter 12

Deep in the forest stood a small hut, topped with woven branches and leaves. As thunder rumbled and the rain hammered down outside, Mitch sat on a tree trunk stool, hunched over a wooden table covered with sword hilts, and a mess of wood scrapings.

"Will we see our friends again?" asked a sorrowful voice from the corner.

Mitch clenched his teeth and gripped hold of a hilt, scraping at it aggressively with a small blade. He hoped not; they were useless to him now and had wasted enough of his time. He kept scratching and scraping until the hilt was thin enough to be snapped in half, then he cast the pieces across the floor and picked up another.

"Are we still doing a new civilisation?"

Mitch answered by scraping harder and faster, and Logan seemed to understand that the conversation was over.

Many more wood scraps fell that day until one undamaged hilt remained on the table. Mitch placed down the blade and raised the last piece of his handiwork. He rotated the object with both hands and admired the carving – a skull within a sun, his symbol for the new kingdom. A falling tear prompted him to continue, so he reached for the knife and continued scraping until Logan's voice spoke from the corner once again. "Someone's coming, Mitch, my friend."

He listened; there were indeed footsteps approaching. He dropped the last hilt and crept towards the door, following the sound along the wall with the point of his knife. The door creaked, and he positioned his blade to greet the face of the intruder. "Halt!" he yelled.

The door swung open to reveal a drenched Sanbon standing in the storm. She ignored the knife and muscled through to escape the rain. "Don't you ever light a fire?" she asked. After tugging at her long hair, wringing it dry, she knelt to retrieve some wood scraps to burn, but then held up some pieces, recognising what they'd once been.

Mitch remained at the door and turned away from Sanbon's concerned eyes. "What's going on?" she asked. "You ran off with the hairless ones and never returned, and now you're destroying your hilts?"

He backed against the wall as she stepped towards him and then raised a halting hand as she opened her arms to embrace him. It pained him to do so, but the chieftain's command was made clear, and still echoed in his mind.

"What's wrong?" Sanbon asked, with a desperate look in her eyes.

Mitch didn't answer. He clutched his knife, cleaning nothing from the shining metal with a firm stroke of the thumb.

"Mitch, we need to fix this now," she said, and she turned to Logan. "There is no place for an Ant in our future together. It's time you made a choice. Me or–"

"Logan," he answered, finishing her sentence without hesitation. "I choose Logan."

He seized the opportunity to provide a perfect excuse. Mitch had never experienced friendship until he found his robot companion, lost and wandering in the forest, and since that day he had always been pleasant and loyal, which was more than could be said about the Skullkrakat. Without making eye contact, Mitch creaked open the door to reveal shadows cast across the forest by the dark clouds. He stepped into the pouring rain, and a puddle soaked his feet.

"Why?" Sanbon asked from behind.

"Don't come here again," Mitch said over his shoulder. He then walked away from the woman he loved, leaving her staring at the empty doorway as part of her died inside.

She knelt to the ground and raised her palms to her face as her eyes filled with tears. "Why?" she whimpered. Her body started to tremble.

She lifted her head to the plodding of heavy feet; Logan stepped past and smiled back at her before trudging off into the rain.

How could this Ant mean so much to him? An enemy in her own home. She carried Mitch's child, but as things stood, he was a danger to the unborn; and for this reason, she'd told nobody, not even her father. Her sights fixed on the open door as she returned to her feet, and she sniffed deeply, wiping the tears from her eyes. Anger rose up through the pain; then she unsheathed her sword and followed.

Chapter 13

"Bernard to Mainframe. Bernard to Mainframe."

"Yes, yes, alright!"

The dome leader waddled through the Outer Zone, huffing and spluttering as a notification flashed in his AR vision and played through his ear implant. He hurried up the steps towards the mainframe door, pausing halfway to catch his breath.

"Bernard to Mainframe."

"Alright!"

He struggled the last few steps, and then with a deep wheeze, he slammed his hand against the panel on the wall. *WHOOOSH.*

"Bernard to Mainframe."

"Shut up!"

He hurried to the inner door. *WHOOOSH.*

After entering the mainframe, he took up position in front of the screen at the left wall, and with a few deep breaths, he straightened his back, adjusted his silver collar, raised his nose, and forced the deepest possible cough.

"Bernard to–"

He gestured his hand, creating a green flash to end the summoning, and then his eyes met with the cold stare of a militant-looking man who's face filled the screen.

"Bernard," the man said in a stern tone.

The dome leader stepped back and turned his head to the side.

"Yes, master," he said, and then he moved his attention to the floor.

"It is disappointing that I must contact you again so soon."

"Disappointing indeed," Bernard mumbled to his feet.

"Things appear to have worsened since our last conversation," the man continued.

The dome leader didn't respond. He raised his eyebrows and pouted at the floor, reluctantly acknowledging the remarks.

"Shall we address each point, Bernard?"

"Oh, shall we?" he answered, followed by a scrunched grin and a vigorous nod.

"Canvas capacity has again decreased. Explain," said the man, failing to detect the sarcasm.

Bernard glanced a brief smile upwards. "Quality is better than quantity, isn't it?"

The man's eyebrows screwed together as his face stared down. "Increase productivity, or there will be serious repercussions," he commanded, in a stricter tone.

The dome leader raised his shoulders and shuddered. "Ooo," he said.

"Next, I have evidence to suggest you have obtained the architectural files for space-grade assistant synthetic humans which are forbidden on your planet. Explain!"

Bernard opened his mouth to answer, then hesitated.

"Answer me, Bernard!"

The dome leader lifted his head a little. "I'm under attack."

"Under attack from who?" the man asked.

Bernard nodded to himself, humming at the floor.

"Under attack from who, Bernard?"

"Not my fault ... not my fault," he muttered in response.

"Bernard, who?"

The old man rocked his head from side to side, pouting at the floor again. "Maz," he said. "Hap, Sanbon, Krakat ... you won't know them, they–"

"Maz?" the man interrupted. "These are not your citizens. Have you been contacting other domes?"

"No," he answered. "The hostility came to me."

Bernard had been observing Mitch. Not even a dome leader can authorise prisoner release, so his once most promising creator would have to accept defeat and return to Canvas where he belonged. With master creator status and possibly still even dome leadership to look forward to, the dome offered him a secure future, the traitor's only realistic future.

The man didn't respond to this revelation but instead moved on to the next point: "I have evidence of structural anomalies in the southern Outer Zone. Explain."

Bernard coughed into his fist and then looked up at the screen. "Sorry, I think I'm due to ask a question, actually," he said. "Do you plan on helping me?"

"I repeat, I have evidence of structural anomalies in the south. Explain."

Bernard laughed. "Well if you're not going to help me, then you'll find out soon enough. Goodbye!" He lifted his hand and powered down the screen.

◇

NOK ... NOK-NOK ... NOK-NOK-NOK.

The door whooshed open, and the boy appeared, swinging his Asher arm. "Ah, chosen one. How can I be of–"

"What did you find in the south?" Mitch asked. "Talk to me, you little cretin."

The boy responded by walloping Mitch's kneecap with a mighty two-handed swing of his toy. *CLONK.* "You're the cretin, chosen one," he said.

Mitch bent over in agony, clutching his leg. "If you weren't so damned useful, I would kill you," he wheezed. "Now what did you find?"

The boy smirked. "Guess," he said.

Mitch growled in frustration, rubbing his knee. "Just tell me!"

The boy laughed. "I found a door to the outside."

Mitch released his leg, forgetting the pain. "What?"

"Let's go outside, chosen one," said the boy.

"You'll burn on the outside," Mitch snapped back.

"No I won't, don't lie. I've seen it!"

Mitch started to panic. If the troublesome child were to spread rumours, it would cause chaos and ruin everything. "You haven't seen anything," he said.

"I have actually. I was in a vent and saw big smiling Ashers, and brown coloured ground outside."

Mitch wanted to call the boy a liar, but he couldn't have dreamt this up. With the dome being the source of the Ants, the danger had now increased, yet an outer door meant a glimpse of hope for his people.

The boy chuckled.

"What's funny?" Mitch asked.

The boy laughed again. "But I can't access that passage with my Asher arm anyway, you idiot."

Mitch lunged at the boy and grabbed his tunic with both hands. "I'll get us outside on one condition," he said.

The boy bubbled with excitement. "Yes, chosen one?"

"When I release the prisoners. You and the disciples get *everyone* to that door. Okay?"

"Yes, chosen one, but when? You take so long with everything," he complained.

"Soon, you little piece of excrement. But until that happens, you don't tell anyone about this, alright?!"

"Yes, chosen one. Hurry up then."

◇

Mitch emerged from the burrow, mumbling to himself as he entered the forest. He paced into the trees, pinching and rubbing his forehead, turning from side-to-side, unsure what to do next. The Skullkrakat prepared for war with the Ants, a war which would lead them to his people; he didn't have much time. A sweep of his hair became a clenched handful. "Codes, codes, codes," he muttered as he headed towards the tunnel entrance. But then he stopped. "Logan!" he yelled, turning to scan the forest. With both hands, he rubbed his face, closing his eyes to listen for the heavy sound of stomping feet. The sound never came.

"Logan!" He paced in circles, searching the distant trees, but with each rotation, he felt more alone. He wandered back to the burrow and checked for movement along the dome wall. "LOGAN!" The cry shredded his throat, but his companion didn't appear. He returned his palms to his closed eyes, but this time not to listen, but to separate himself from reality. The darkness was comforting, although his thoughts were not: a door without codes, the loss of the woman he loved, a failed dome alliance, and a new and dangerous enemy – the Skullkrakat. Vulnerable in the absence of his best friend, he wished to hide in the dark forever, never to face the world again.

◇

"Bel to Mainframe. Bel to Mainframe."

Bel walked calmly up the steps to the mainframe door as the notification flashed in her AR vision and played through her ear implant.

"Bel to Mainframe."

She placed her hand against the panel. *WHOOOSH*. She then strolled casually through the white room and raised her hand to the second. *WHOOOSH*.

"Bel to Mainframe."

"Yes, okay!" she said with a gentle laugh.

She positioned herself at the screen on the left wall, gestured her hand, and with a green flash, a large stern face appeared.

"Bel."

Bel's welcoming smile adorned her face as she greeted the man with a calm nod. "Hello, sir. How are you?" she asked.

"I am well," he answered.

"Good," said Bel with another nod.

The supervisor rarely made contact, but when he did, it would be to congratulate her on the dome's exceptional achievements in Canvas. For that reason, she stood with a proud smile, ready to absorb the compliments.

"It is disappointing that I must contact you," he said.

Bel's smile dropped. She opened her mouth to question him, but then he continued.

"I have evidence to suggest you have been in contact with another dome. Explain."

A wave of dizziness rushed over her. The supervisor couldn't possibly have found out. "No, it's not like that sir," she said, trying not to panic. "Another dome contacted *us*. I haven't broken any rules. I can assure you."

The man screwed his eyebrows. "Name those who made contact."

"Mitch. Just a man named Mitch," she answered, desperate to cooperate.

"I am aware of the involvement of Maz and a threat of hostility towards the other dome. Explain," he said.

Bel gasped. "No, no, no. There are no hostilities," she assured him. "Mitch wants to evacuate his people because he believes his dome is killing them. He's seeking–" And then it struck her. "Sir ..." she said, "if you could provide security override codes and details of any safe evacuation points, he could save them from harm, and there would be no reason left for him to contact us. Everything can return to normal here, and I will never speak of this to anyone. I promise you." She found the whole situation desperately uncomfortable and wished it gone for good. "All my citizens are present," she added for assurance. "This will not affect my community. You can be sure of that, sir." Her heart raced as she awaited a response.

"I will give you what he needs," the supervisor concluded. "But there are conditions."

◇

The moisture from the wet ground soaked into Mitch's trousers as he sat near the burrow, hugging his knees tight to his chest. A distant sound then caught his attention, and he peeled his face away from his wrapped arm. The sun breaking through the clouds stabbed at his eyes, so with a hand as a shield, he gazed along the wall of the dome. "Logan?" He closed his blurry eyes to sense the direction of the sound; the footsteps were too fast for the robot, so he jumped to his feet. He considered running, but with no clear plan, he didn't know where. Foggy thoughts clouded his mind, and he struggled to make connections, but it was no use. He returned to the darkness of his palms and surrendered himself to fate.

"Mitch!" a voice cried.

He lowered his hands as Sanbon approached, rushing beside the dome with her blade drawn. With Logan missing, this was no coincidence.

"What have you done," he whispered to himself, with a wave of anger starting to rise.

Sanbon stepped up to him and sheathed her sword. "Mitch, my love. Listen." She hugged him tight, but he kept his arms firmly by his sides; killing his feelings now would be a sacrifice for his survival. "Mitch, everything will be okay now. Trust me." But it would not be okay. She was foolish to think that destroying Logan would solve the problems they faced.

Mitch crept his hand until his fingertips met with the grooves of his carving.

"You should have listened to me, my love."

"Listened to what?" Mitch asked as he wrapped his hand around the sword's hilt.

"Logan ... he *is* one of them."

In one swift movement, Mitch unsheathed the sword and jumped back, raising the sharp edge to her neck. "What did you do with him?"

"Mitch ... I ... nothing–"

"What did you do?"

He backed away, with the blade still aimed at her face. "Stay away," he said, stepping back into the trees. "And if you reveal the location of my hut to *anyone*, I will slice them into a hundred pieces!"

Then he ran.

◊

Hap grinned with anticipation. "Load file, Hap, narwhal one, version one."

In a sudden assault to the retina, the dark void of Canvas filled with blue light and Maz found herself standing in an ocean, deep beneath the surface.

"This is weird," she said.

Hap was now a Viking warrior, with a horned helmet on his head and a drinking horn in his hand. Maz was okay with this, but she wasn't okay with the braided beard hanging from his chin.

"Where is it?" she asked.

Hap turned in a circle. "Ah, there!"

Shapes became visible in the distant blue.

"They're coming ..." said Hap.

After a short but worthwhile wait, six majestic creatures drifted over them.

"Whales with horns, like sea unicorns!" Maz gasped, captivated by the view.

"Well, that's where you're wrong," said Hap with a smug face.

Maz focused on his eyes, not the beard. "Go on," she sighed.

"It's not a horn. It's a long tooth!" He appeared very pleased with himself.

Maz shook her head. "You're stupid. I'm out of here. I need to get back to my project."

"It is!" yelled Hap. "And why are you bothering with your project? Bel will change her mind. You wait and see."

"Hap, she doesn't have the codes," Maz argued. "I wish things had gone better, but there's nothing we can do. We failed the mission."

The Viking twisted his beard, thoughtfully. "Why don't we head out anyway?" he asked. "He'll have another idea, won't he? And I quite liked the forest."

"And you think he'll need us now?" Maz asked. "Just following him around?"

"No, I guess not," Hap said with a frown.

The adventure beyond the dome walls had been a great privilege, and for that, Maz would be forever thankful to Mitch. She wished it didn't have to end so soon, yet she was grateful for the experience. If the quality of life outside were better, she would be tempted to leave now and never come back. But as things stood, they wouldn't last long in the forest without Mitch to guide them, and he owed them nothing. As she gazed into the virtual blue ocean, she considered that maybe, one day, she would escape the dome and explore the old world again. Perhaps by then, a successful Mitch would welcome them back.

"Maz to Mainframe."

She gasped at the sound from her ear implant.

"I told you, I knew it!" Hap shouted, turning to her with explosive excitement.

"You got that as well?" she asked.

"Yes!" he cried, and the ocean disappeared, leaving an empty black void.

"Eject," said Maz, and the pod around her sprung open, dropping her to a squatted position on the floor. She squinted in the light and then hurried for her tunic, ignoring the hatch as her nutrients weren't due.

As the platform descended, Hap leapt from the eastern path and sprinted with great enthusiasm across the grass beneath her. Maz caught up with him at the Outer Zone gateway behind her block, where he stood beckoning her to hurry.

They shot into the corridor. Maz was too excited to recall or recite each stage of the Ash-bot's directions, but her visual memory had formed well, and moments later, they stamped up the steps to the mainframe door. Maz raised her hand. *WHOOOSH*. They almost lodged themselves in the doorway as they barged through at the same time, but in the next room, Maz hurried ahead. *WHOOOSH*.

"You have the codes?" she gasped as she staggered inside.

Bel turned from the centre screen with a hand across her chest. Despite once again being startled, she seemed in good spirits. "Yes, my angel," she said with a warm smile.

The words sprung Hap into the air. "Yes! Yes!" he yelled, shaking his fists.

The mission was back on, and Maz couldn't wait to deliver the news to Mitch, finally proving their worth.

"But there are conditions," Bel added.

Conditions? Maz thought. Bel's change in expression suggested the celebration would be short-lived.

Chapter 14

Once again, Maz found her bare feet on the fallen leaves of the forest. She ignored Hap as he stepped in irregular patterns, aiming for the big crunchy ones.

"Will she really seal the tree when we get back?" he asked.

"She only wants what's best for us."

"And you believe a system update in our dome will clear the threat?"

"I hope so," said Maz.

"So why are The Elite allowing Mitch's people out, but we have to go back?" Hap asked. "Don't you think that's unfair?"

It didn't seem fair, and something didn't feel right, but for now, only the mission mattered to Maz. If Mitch succeeded today and a new civilisation went ahead, there would be a difficult decision to make. Bel trusted them to return, but nothing prevented them from breaking that promise.

Earlier that morning, they braved a visit to the Skullkrakat. To their relief, Gakit and Tamak were off duty, but the residence was empty. Sanbon seemed happy to see them when they found her at the armoury, but she explained it was over, and that Mitch had lost his mind. She warned them to keep their distance, but on learning they had obtained the codes, she provided directions to his secret hut in the forest. She wished them luck, suggesting they approach with caution, and she left the room in quite a hurry.

"There's the corner of the mound," said Maz. "It should be—yes there!"

A hut came into view among the trees, like those in the new village, but with no stilts and no fence for protection. They circled to locate the door, which creaked open as they approached, and a long sword poked out to greet them, followed by atrociously messed up hair, and a pair of grey, puffy eyes.

"You have the codes?" Mitch asked in a dry and damaged voice.

They entered the one room to find it littered with a mess of wood pieces and scrapings. Mitch dropped to a stool and slumped over a severely mutilated wooden table. He beckoned them to join, but Maz hesitated. This was not the same passionate man they left behind.

"Are we too late?" she asked.

Mitch forced a slight smile. "No. Thank you."

The friends took a seat and admired the carnage around them while waiting for the news to sink in. The state of the table hinted as to where Mitch's energy had gone, but he soon found more after learning Sanbon had revealed his location. He ran out of the door, pointing his sword towards the trees, and stamping footsteps circled the hut three times.

He returned to his seat and thrust out a hand. "Give me the codes."

Maz reached into her tunic pocket and handed him the scrunched-up piece of material. He unravelled the map over the least damaged part of the table, then flipped it over to reveal a long list of codes scribbled on the reverse. His eyes gaped.

"The domes have a hidden outer door in the south," Maz advised him. "The codes will open that door, and there's a self-destruct code too. You've been ordered to destroy the dome, to ensure the future safety of your people."

"With pleasure," he said. "But Bel doesn't give me orders."

Maz explained to him that the codes were provided by The Elite, who remained in secret contact with the dome leaders. The supervisor demanded their immediate return and was already descending for a routine data transfer and a system update to protect them from the same threat.

Mitch didn't speak for some time. His opinion of The Elite was well known to them, but there may not be another chance to act.

"Oh, and Max," Hap added.

"Oh yes," said Maz. "Not from the Elite, but Bel asked whether you'd met a man called Max out here?"

Mitch's eyebrows tensed from interrupted thought, but then he shook his head in response.

Maz also wanted to question Logan's absence, but following Sanbon's warning of caution, she kept quiet on the subject, hoping Hap would do the same.

Mitch eventually rose to his feet. "It's time."

Chapter 15

In the quiet garden of Mitch's dome, three serious faces peered around the big tree.

"Come on you idiots. It's clear!"

They ran across the lawn and stopped on the terrace to psyche themselves up. "This is it," said Mitch, bouncing a fist. "Stick to the plan and avoid the Ashers."

Maz's heart raced as he led them through the Outer Zone, taking the familiar corridors until he diverted into the side passage. *NOK ... NOK-NOK ... NOK-NOK-NOK*. The door whooshed open, and the boy appeared, holding the arm of an Ash-bot.

"It's time," said Mitch.

The boy's face lit up. He jumped through the doorway two-footed and stretched his Ash-bot arm as high as he could reach. "Yeeuurrss!" he cried. With a thump to Mitch's leg, he bounced past and into the main corridor.

"I should've brought the sword," Mitch muttered.

The boy hummed to himself, swinging his toy, as the team made their way towards the town circle. As they approached the gateway, they passed the door where the Ash-bots had abducted the man on their previous visit. The boy hopped over, held the robot arm to the panel, and the door slid open. "Come on!" he whispered inside.

Mitch stormed over and grabbed the arm off him. "Not yet!" he growled, and he raised it again to reseal the door. "We need to release *all* the doors and pods together, or we'll look suspicious!"

The boy snatched the arm back. "Well hurry up then."

Maz crept through the gateway and peered around the town circle, paying careful attention to the nearby Vegetation Zone where the Ash-bot lurked previously. They were alone, from what she could make out, so Mitch huddled them together for instructions.

"Right, so here's the plan ..."

They all leaned in.

"Boy."

"Yes, chosen one."

"The moment I say, you must round up the remaining disciples and prepare to direct *all* citizens to the escape route you discovered. Okay?"

The boy nodded. "Yes, chosen one."

"And where is that?" Mitch asked.

The boy pointed south. "Left gateway," he said. "At the end of the main corridor, the door on the right won't open. Behind that leads to the outside door."

"Good," Mitch replied. "I'll open those doors. Send *everyone* that way."

"Yes, chosen one." The boy started wandering down the path towards the north block.

"Not yet!" Mitch yelled. "Right, Maz."

"Yes?"

"Once I'm inside the mainframe, stand at the left gateway in the south. The boy will direct people to you."

"Okay," she said with a nod.

"Hap."

"Yes, chosen one," he answered with a grin.

The boy giggled and rasped his lips, but Mitch wasn't amused.

"Go past Maz to the end of the main corridor," he said. "When the locked door opens, direct everyone down the final passage to the exit."

"Yes, ch–" Maz gave him a stern glance. "Yes ... I can do that."

Mitch reached into his tunic pocket. "As soon as the escape route is obvious to the flow of citizens, I need you both at the front. The boy and I will make sure the last of them follow."

He crouched and unravelled a sheet of material on the grey path beneath his feet; it was another map, more faded than the last, showing a single dome and its immediate surroundings. He pointed to the south wall marked with an S, circled a little to the west, and ran his finger from that position to a mound. "Lead them directly across the dusty terrain and into the tree line," he said. "Inside the forest, you'll soon reach this mound. Don't miss the angle!" He was becoming agitated. "Follow the mound left, that's *left,* to the end. Got that?!"

Maz nodded as Mitch stuffed the material back into his tunic pocket.

"There's a tunnel entrance where everyone can shelter for the first night, but it's hard to find, so wait for me after the mound," he said. "I'm sure that will be far enough from the explosion."

Maz gazed across the town circle towards her position in the south; her role was easy enough. Mitch then set off, and they rushed down the first path, but instead of taking the direct route past the printer column, he led them behind the north block, and across the grass to behind the west block. No Ash-bots or humans were visible around the central courtyard, so the long route seemed unnecessary, but they soon reached the first of the two southern gateways – the way to the mainframe.

"So, you're sure it's this way?" Mitch asked.

"Yes," Maz answered. "Everything is the same."

"You'd better be right about this. Let's go."

Maz rushed into the corridor, leading the way, and as with the garden route, every passage was the same as back home. She was delighted beyond words when at the top of the steps, they reached a door marked 'Mainframe'.

Mitch's feet stamped back and forth behind her as she raised a shaking hand. Her attention locked on the panel, but then Hap gasped as a red hand-print appeared before them.

"Why isn't it open yet?" said an angry voice from behind.

Maz turned and snatched the Ash-bot arm from the boy, who wasn't best pleased. She held it to the panel, which again flashed red. Her heart thumped in her chest as Hap turned to her with worried eyes. Mitch stopped pacing and watched them as they backed away towards the steps.

The boy laughed and swiped the arm back from Maz. "Only the dome leader can enter the mainframe," he said. "The disciples already tried this door." He giggled at Mitch's stressed face.

"You lot are useless," he said. He took heavy breaths as his face grew redder.

"You're useless," said the boy. "You're meant to be the chosen one, but you can't do anything." He scurried away as Mitch stepped forward with tightly clenched fists.

"I *am* the chosen one," he hissed, approaching the panel. "I *am* the chosen one," he said again. "I've always known it. I have a purpose greater than all the rest." He raised a hand. "And *nothing* will stop me." WHOOOSH.

He studied his hand in disbelief. "I *am* the chosen one?" he whispered. He stared through the open door, and his face hardened. "I *am* the chosen one!" His head and chest rose high like a gallant leader, and he disappeared swiftly through the doorway.

The boy sniggered as he followed.

"Don't tell him I'm a chosen one too," Maz whispered to Hap, and they both chuckled as they entered the small white room and passed through the second door.

Mitch studied the screens, pinching his chin over folded arms. "Come on, which is it?" he asked.

"The middle screen is for inside, for surveillance," Maz advised, pointing forwards. "The left one is for outside, for communication with The Elite—no, don't bother. It's for incoming communication only."

Mitch stopped before he reached the screen. He turned and pointed to the third. "And that one?" he asked.

"To control the dome," Maz answered.

Mitch crossed the face of the central screen and stepped up to the system screen. The blank surface flashed green from a wave of the hand, and he reached into his tunic pocket. "Go!" he yelled. He unravelled the sheet of material, hung it over his arm, and glanced down the list of codes.

◊

In the town circle, Maz, Hap and the boy rushed out from the corridor and turned right. They hurried along the Vegetation Zone until they reached the other southern gateway and stopped to survey their surroundings.

"Right," said Maz, panting for breath. "The doors should start—" A heavy, shrill sound from the direction of the town centre interrupted her, and she stepped across the grass until she could see past the nearby south block. Citizens were beginning to appear on their ledges on the north block opposite.

"It's open," she said. "He's done it!"

She turned to speak to the boy, but he'd already disappeared.

◊

Mitch studied the codes. The next read: !ACSYSD#84EBUA. He tapped it into the screen's touch surface. *TAP ... TAP-TAP ...* "Authorisation code?" he mumbled to himself. *TAP-TAP-TAP ... TAP ...* "Number eighty-four? Dome number eighty-four, I guess?"

◊

Maz started yelling and beckoning the distant citizens towards her position, and as she did so, the harsh noise sounded in the east. The dark surfaces of the block slid open, and from where she stood, she could see people dropping from their pods.

"Run to me as soon as you can," Hap said, placing a hand on her shoulder.

Maz wrapped her arms around him. "I won't lose you," she said. They squeezed each other tight, and then she pushed him towards the gateway. "Go!"

Hap hurried to the path and rushed away into the corridor, but immediately he returned, stepping back onto the grass as an aged man with a white beard emerged from inside.

"So, we have visitors," he said. The silver collar identified him as Mitch's dome leader.

"Sorry, sir," said Maz. "We'll be leaving in a moment."

"Oh good," he said, clapping his hands. "Are you leaving alone, or is today the big day?"

They all flinched as the unlocking of the south block almost deafened them, and more naked bodies started dropping from their pods. The dome leader smiled and rubbed his hands together with what appeared to be a genuine expression of excitement. "Oh good!" he said. "Today *is* the big day! Congratulations to Mitch!"

◇

The fourth code read: !ACSYSD#84WBUA. *TAP ... TAP-TAP ... TAP-TAP-TAP ...* "System?" Mitch mumbled to himself. "Dome number eighty-four." *TAP ... TAP ... TAP-TAP ...* "West block ..."

◇

Maz observed with curiosity as the dome leader stepped off the path and waddled away across the grass towards the other south gateway, singing to himself.

"Will he stop Mitch?" Hap asked. "What should we do?"

Maz was unsure if the old man posed any threat, but then the shrill sound rang out from the west. "Quick, go!" she said, and Hap headed to his position.

Citizens now flowed down the block walls in high numbers, gathering around the buildings and chattering to one another. Maz waved and shouted, "This way!" gaining the attention of many, but the majority seemed bemused and hesitant to acknowledge her. She became annoyed with them; maybe they deserved to die from stupidity. They were no different from those she avoided back home, but this was unexpected; they were not suffering or desperate to escape.

◇

The next code read: !ACSYSD#84EOUA. *TAP ... TAP-TAP ... TAP-TAP-TAP ... TAP ... TAP ... TAP-TAP ...* Mitch paused to think. "East outer," he mumbled. "Unlock all?" *TAP-TAP-TAP-TAP.*

◇

The town circle became chaotic. Mitch could not fail after everything they'd been through, so Maz left the gateway and sprinted past every block, screaming to announce an emergency and for all citizens to evacuate south. She reminded herself that these people were unprepared for a situation like this. And for that reason, she held her temper and encouraged the crowds until they at last began moving.

◇

The final code read: !ACSYSD#84SD@1CS. *TAP ... TAP-TAP ... TAP-TAP-TAP ... TAP ... TAP ... TAP-TAP ...* "Self-destruct," he mumbled. *TAP-TAP.* He stroked his chin. *A measurement of time,* he thought. *One.* "One centisegment?" He threw the material to the floor and stepped back from the screen. "One damned centisegment?" It wasn't anywhere near enough time to evacuate – the supervisor had deceived them.

"Elite scum," he spat, marching to the opposite screen. "I knew it." He raised his hand and produced a green flash. The supervisor wasn't descending for a system update; he was descending to ensure the silencing of two rebellions. "Call," he commanded. "Call space." The surface remained blank. "Call The Elite ... open communication, connect to The Elite, connect to space, emergency, danger, emergency call, emergency call-back, answer me you scum!" He pummelled the unresponsive black surface, then marched back to the system screen, clawing at his scalp. They needed time to reach the mound, but not enough time for the dome to retaliate. *Thirty-five*, he decided. *TAP ... TAP-TAP ... TAP-TAP.*

The room sank into a deep, blinking red.

Mitch set a countdown timer in his AR vision, and as it started ticking down, he took a long breath and strode towards the door. "Time to finish this," he said.

He raised his hand to the panel. *WHOOOSH*. But on the other side stood Bernard, with a darkness in his eyes.

The leader snarled through his white beard and stepped through the doorway, turning to the inside panel as the last of the green hand-print faded away. "They must've chosen you already," he said. "But you've ruined that now, haven't you?"

Mitch backed away.

Bernard moved deeper into the beating heart of the dome. His eyes widened to each pulse, revealing a hint of fear. "What have you done?" he asked.

Mitch chose his moment, sprinting past his leader and through the open doorway behind. He stopped and turned. "I had no choice, Bernard," he said. "The dome is dangerous. If you hurry now, you can save yourself."

Bernard let out a howl of laughter. "Dangerous?" he said, then he coughed violently.

"Yes," Mitch answered. "There are dangerous Ashers, large–"

"Oh, the Ants!" Bernard interrupted. "Like your *best friend*." He grinned fiendishly. "And it's a shame you've also lost Sanbon," he added. "I enjoyed watching her, especially."

Mitch's thoughts flashed back to the bedroom, and the passionate, intimate moments he and Sanbon had shared. He ran his hand down the alluring curves of her smooth body and turned towards the doorway, where the curtain scrunched at one side. Beyond the waves of textile, in the dim orange flicker of the passage, was Logan's smiling face, as he learnt about being a person. Mitch heard Sanbon's voice, as though she were by his side: *"I don't like it when he watches us, Mitch."*

"It was *you*." Mitch's focus on his grinning leader was as sharp as two pointing daggers. "You've been watching me all this time!" He stepped back into the mainframe, trembling at first, but then exploded forward and grabbed Bernard around the throat, digging his nails into the fat, wrinkled skin of his cold neck. The old man choked and struggled as Mitch pushed him back until his head slammed into the centre screen. Mitch then smashed the old man's head against the surface repeatedly. *THUMP! THUMP! THUMP!* "Get out of him!" he screamed. *THUMP! THUMP!* "What have you done with him!"

Cracks started appearing on the monitor, and Mitch's eyes became flooded with tears. He released his hold and Bernard crumpled on the floor, with trails of fresh blood creeping through his grey hair. The dome leader raised his haggard eyes to Mitch, wincing with pain. "How does it feel, to lose what you held so dear ... now we *both* know that feeling, don't we?"

Mitch waved a clenched fist, ready to silence him.

"You don't understand, do you?" said Bernard. "For the first time in the history of our species, we have guaranteed nutrients, shelter, a healthy next generation." He croaked to clear his throat and wiped a stream of blood from his temple. "No predators, no life-threatening disease, no hostility or invasion. Don't you see?"

Mitch checked his countdown.

"But Mitch wants to rewind all human achievement and become a primate in the forest, back where we started."

"You're forgetting something, Bernard," he answered. "We *are* primates, and primates don't belong in machines."

Then with a final strike, Bernard's head dropped to the floor.

Mitch ran through the corridors towards the town circle, glancing down junctions for any stragglers as he passed. He came running out of the gateway and smiled at the sight of the open blocks. But something wasn't right; too many people were crowded around Maz's position. He shouldered his way through the loitering citizens until he reached the other gateway. Maz had moved on, but the people were standing around, confused.

"Go!" he shouted, pointing down the corridor towards Hap's position, but nobody moved, something was wrong. The Ash-bots were not the problem – one lay nearby with a red blinking head, and three citizens sat on it. "Move!" he yelled at the crowd, but the only response was a few turning bald heads.

"Ah, chosen one." The boy emerged from the direction of the gateway, weaving between tunics. "Good work, chosen one," he said chuckling to himself.

"What?" Mitch asked.

"You didn't open the last door, did you?"

Mitch panicked, glancing at the countdown. He'd entered all the codes; there were no more.

The boy giggled at him.

◊

Maz and Hap knelt on the ground, holding each other tight, as the exit door remained sealed closed beside them. Confused citizens filled the corridor, waiting for something to happen, having no idea their deaths could be imminent.

"I don't want to die," Hap whispered.

"He hasn't finished," Maz assured him. But in truth, she feared the worst. The dome leader didn't look tough enough to overpower Mitch, but something must have happened. *I must go back*. She let go of her friend, but before she stood, another door opened.

WHOOOSH. TRUDGE TRUDGE TRUDGE.

A line of Ants emerged from the room, with smiles beaming, delighted to meet everyone. The people retreated up the corridor in panic, colliding and falling over one another.

Hap stepped in front of Maz and raised his fists to protect her as the robots ploughed through the screaming crowd, hurling citizens against the walls, floor and ceiling. "Stay down!" he shouted, as one of the Ants turned to confront him. "I'm your new friend," he said, but the robot didn't reply. He raised his fists further, but the Ant stomped forward, reached around his hands, and grabbed him by the shoulders. Hap struggled hard, thumping at the Ant's massive grey arms. "Maz, run!" he cried, but there was nowhere to go.

Maz cowered in the grip of fear as the Ant wrapped its strong arms around her friend, squeezing him from behind until his face turned red and he gasped for breath. She screamed in terror as he kicked and struggled to break free, but the robot's strength overwhelmed him. Maz was powerless to help, so she curled into a ball to play dead, but as her eyes closed, she heard a loud *SWOOOSH*, followed by a piercing *CLANG* and a heavy *THUMP* on the ground.

She opened her eyes. Hap crouched beside the decapitated body of the Ant, gasping for air, and above him, in the wide-open exit, stood the tall figure of Sanbon, raising her large, glistening blade.

Krakat stepped into the doorway, lowering a severed Ant arm from the outer wall. The sun shined against his rugged face for the first time, and he turned to the dusty terrain, where many more warriors of the darkness had surfaced and were hacking at a scattering of fallen Ants. The chieftain dropped the robot arm, tensed his body and raised his scarred face to the sky. Then with a mighty roar, the Skullkrakat lowered their weapons and turned.

"At last!" Gakit shouted, pointing his spear to the dome. The horde of warriors revealed their teeth and set off in a ground-shaking stampede.

"Get down!" Sanbon screamed into the corridor.

Maz ducked her head as the staunch figure of Krakat shot past her, wielding his blade. Many more Skullkrakat followed, flying through the passage, leaping over citizens as they swung their weapons and sliced the Ants to pieces. Tamak slurred complaints as he struggled to step over the whimpering bald heads as nimbly as the others. "Leave some for me," he said.

Maz crawled to Hap and helped him up. "Come on. We need to go." She turned to the crowd. "This way, hurry!" she yelled, and the bewildered citizens began clambering to their feet.

They ran straight at the tree line without looking back. Maz could hear the patter of footsteps behind, so with the blast imminent, she sprinted as fast as she could to the safety of the forest.

◊

Back at the gateway, Mitch stood dangling the irritating child by the leg.

"Get your hands off me, chosen one!" he giggled. "You've got a door to open."

Mitch stared down the corridor at the Ants causing mayhem. "Here's one for you!" he yelled. "Come and get this one!"

The boy struggled, laughing hysterically. "Stop it, chosen one. Let me go!" Then suddenly, he dropped to the path with a thud, and Mitch froze.

At the far end of the corridor, Krakat charged through the junction and sliced an Ant clean in half with his blade. Mitch took a step back from the gateway. "He's come for me. The war has begun." More warriors followed, and citizens cowered as chunks of robot whistled past their heads. Krakat then started waving people to the next passage. *The door is open. He's not killing them.* The last few Ash-bots set off in a bouncing pursuit, but their bleating danger reports soon silenced, and the corridor became a calm river of robotic limbs and fidgeting torsos.

The chieftain glanced towards the gateway with his dark, predatory eyes. He sheathed his sword and walked away, beckoning Mitch to follow.

"He trusts me," Mitch whispered. "It must be a rescue."

He turned to face the town circle. The surfaces on the blocks were open, the pods empty.

He hadn't noticed the boy was missing until he scurried up the side of the nearby block. "Can't see anyone else," he said. "You did it chosen one."

Mitch moved his hands to his hips, turned away, and took a deep breath to conceal his emotion. "Go–" he said. "Go. Run!"

The boy hurried through the gateway and into the corridor, swinging his Asher arm to the whooping sounds of victory.

Mitch stepped across the grass for a good view of the central courtyard. The dome seemed so peaceful now. His citizens were free, and he'd make damned sure they're never trapped in a machine again. The weight on his shoulders lifted, and he took another deep breath and smiled. The mission was a success.

◇

In the mainframe, Bernard stood squinting at the communication screen. "Productivity is down again, you say?" He winced, clutching his bleeding head. "Well, sir, there must be a mistake. We've been *particularly* productive of late. Would you like to see?" He turned an ear to the shiny blank surface. "You would? How wonderful!"

◊

Mitch kicked an Ant head aside as he stepped from the corridor to the dusty ground outside. He grinned at the sight of more fallen robots and picked up an arm, which he swiped across the outer wall until it met with the hidden access panel. *SWOOOSH*. He stepped back and admired the closed door. *Clever,* he thought. It was as seamless as the nutrients hatch but marked with a large scratch.

He squinted across the clearing to check for the trail and spotted Sanbon and Krakat waiting at the edge of the forest. Still wary, he took a few steps forward and strained his vision again to read their faces, but something stunned him; the chieftain rested a hand against his daughter's abdomen and placed a kiss on her head. *It's not possible*, he thought. He took a moment to squat on the ground and take it all in. *I do have seed. I'm going to be a father. That's why Krakat is helping me.* With eyes on his love, he rose to his feet, but then–*SWOOOSH*.

"Mitch!" Sanbon screamed from a distance, as her father wrestled her back.

Mitch turned. In the open doorway stood his best friend.

"Logan. Where have you been?" he asked, but the robot smiled in silence.

Sanbon and Krakat stalked across the clearing with long strides and blades drawn, and for a moment, Mitch felt protective. "But Bernard will be gone now," he whispered. "No!" he said, thumping his head. "No. I'm not an idiot!"

The face of his love became clearer as she approached. He gazed into her beautiful eyes and made the decision he should have made a long time ago. "Logan," he said. "I've missed you ... but–"

"I've missed you too, Mitch, my friend."

Tears almost fell, but he fought them back. "Logan, I'm sorry, but I must choose–"

But his words were cut short by the sound of scraping metal, and two long blades burst out from his ribcage. He stared down as a sea of red flooded across his white tunic and a throbbing agony ripped through his soul.

I love you, he intended to say in response to Sanbon's piercing scream, but only the gurgling of blood spoke from his lips.

Logan hoisted him into the air, and once the skewered body became limp, the robot swung his bladed arms down, leaving Mitch's body twitching in the dust until lifeless.

Sanbon struggled and seethed as her father held her back. "This one is different," he growled. "This one we shouldn't face."

More Ants trudged out from the corridor, forming a row of smiles across the dome wall. Logan stepped out in front, raised his blades to the sky, then the other robots lifted their arms in unison, and a chorus of scraping metal rang out.

Sanbon and Krakat turned and ran, shooting into the forest like arrows and bolting through the trees. They sprinted as fast as they could but didn't meet the mound.

"We've missed it!" Krakat roared.

Sanbon glanced back as her legs powered forward beneath her. It was too late to turn around now; Logan was in pursuit, followed by a trail of blades, held wide like wings.

The vegetation thickened around them. Sanbon's leg muscles burned, and her lungs throbbed in her chest. They slowed to a stop, gasping for breath, and as the Ant troop approached, thrashing at the foliage, she and her father raised their swords to greet them.

◇

At the end of the mound, the people gathered, and the last and most weary had caught up and sat on the forest floor to recover. A small group of citizens, many with hair, turned their tunics inside out to reveal a large sun symbol, now displayed across their chests. "Come and hear the good news!" one shouted, addressing the crowd. Maz guessed they were the disciples of whom Mitch spoke.

The Skullkrakat left for the tunnels, but Maz held the dome citizens back to await their new leader.

"Do you think he's here somewhere?" Hap asked.

"Go and search the crowd," Maz answered. "I'll watch the mound."

Hap turned to hurry away, but Maz called him back.

"You were brave back there," she said. "Thank you." She leaned in and kissed his soft lips.

Hap looked stunned, but then a huge smile broke through. He tried to speak but found no words.

◇

Across the forest, Sanbon and Krakat readied themselves for battle, but a thunderous roar then bellowed through the trees as a large, flaming spear launched from the dome, leaving behind a thick, white cloud which engulfed the area beneath. Sanbon gazed for a moment with fascination but had no time to consider its purpose. The trail of Ants had dispersed and formed a circle around them, preventing any route of escape.

Back-to-back, she and her father rotated with blades raised, as the robots approached from all directions through the arriving, sweeping mist.

The enemy outnumbered them, yet as a warrior of the Skullkrakat, Sanbon felt no fear. The point of her blade found its target, and she bared her teeth at the smiling face she so loathed. A splattering of red liquid across the dented head was the last she would know of the heart stolen from hers, and she wasn't falling on this day without taking vengeance first.

◇

At the mound, Maz wiped her lips with the back of her hand as she watched the missile disappear into the blue sky.

"Witness the power of the chosen one!" declared one of the disciples. The crowd gazed up in silence.

Maz understood missiles from the data-banks and realised that the structure in the southern section of Mitch's dome must have been a launch facility. *But why?* she wondered, concerned about Bel and the new village.

"What was that?" Hap asked, but a mighty explosion then tore through the trees, announcing Mitch's victory and throwing everyone to the ground with an unseen, brutal force.

◇

Across the forest, Krakat staggered over to Sanbon as she attempted to raise her dazed head. All around them, fallen Ants flashed red, crying out in a deranged chorus of damaged warnings.

BEEP BEEP BEEP danger report danger BEEP calibration error danger report danger BEEP BEEP report error report danger BEEP...

The chieftain helped his daughter to her feet and suggested they move soon to find the hairless ones. She regained her footing and turned to the sky again as another sound rumbled in the distance. "Did you hear that?" she asked.

Krakat didn't answer. He worked his way through the Ants, silencing them with his sword.

Sanbon stepped through the mist until she stood over Logan, who smiled up at her, moving his legs ineffectively. "... BEEP danger ... sorry, BEEP Mitch my BEEP danger report ..."

She reached down, wiped some blood from the dented head and lifted her shirt to smear a red sun symbol across her abdomen. "Your greatness shall live on," she whispered, and she positioned her blade across Logan's neck. "How does it *feel* ... to be reduced to a pile of scrap." The sword rose high, and following a loud shriek, the smiling head rolled away.

Silence returned to the forest, and Sanbon began to weep; she should have ended it a long time ago.

Chapter 16

A light hum resonated in the sky above Bel's dome as a small craft hovered in the airspace. Inside, the supervisor sat rigid on a single pilot's throne, between smooth metallic, expressionless surfaces. A front window revealed the green expanse, populated by pockets of obedient creators.

A new alert appeared on the glass, obscuring his view.

UPLOAD COMPLETE - PROJECTS SAVED

"Thank you, Bel. Initiate download. One centisegment self-destruct trigger."

The front window then lost its transparency and pulsed red. An alarm cried out as another alert flashed up before him.

WARNING – INCOMING MISSILE DETECTED

The supervisor slammed down his fists.

"Bernard!"

◇

Bel stood at the central courtyard, cradling the baby Bob in her arms, as three of her citizens keenly shared details of their latest Canvas projects with her. She loved hearing their ideas and sharing her suggestions with them, but on this occasion, the pleasant conversation was cut short when a mighty boom shook the dome.

The citizens stopped chattering and gasped. "What was that?" one of them asked.

Bel knew it was the destruction of Mitch's dome, but the recent events would remain secret and *never* affect her community. "Excuse me," she said. "I'll go and check the system. I'm certain it's nothing to worry about." She strolled off towards the mainframe as the bald heads nodded, showing no sign of panic.

Bel headed up the path, smiling to herself, knowing that her dearest Maz and Hap had succeeded. She was very proud of them, but a little worried about their extended absence. To avoid any further damage to her reputation, she'd led the supervisor to believe that the pair were safely back in their pods.

At the Outer Zone gateway, a muffled boom stopped her in her tracks. "Shh, shh, shh," she whispered, bouncing the sleeping baby. The force didn't shake the dome, but Bel was sure the noise was a second explosion. *Strange,* she thought, stepping into the corridor. She made her way towards the mainframe, but another sound alerted her: the clunking of fallen debris, striking the dome's high ceiling and clattering away down the walls.

Moments later, silence returned to the dome.

Bel hurried to the mainframe and arrived at the communication screen.

"Status," she said.

FILE TRANSFER - DOWNLOAD READY

"Accept."

She waited for the system update to commence.

The screen remained blank.

"Accept," she said again.

ERROR - CHECK CONNECTION

"This is strange," she whispered. "Connection status."

NO ACTIVE CONNECTIONS

Chapter 17

Five days later, Mitch's people were hard at work with the Skullkrakat, expanding the new village borders. Huts raised from the dirt at an incredible speed, as increasing numbers of citizens learnt the skills required for inanimate design projects of the physical world. Most seemed to adapt quite well; some hammering, some chopping, but some still gawped weirdly, attempting to comprehend their new existence.

In the centre of the village, Sanbon lifted a stripped tree trunk into a deep hole without asking for assistance. It stood once more, now raising a large metal sun, shining with the actual sun's reflection. Forged as a tribute to the great man they lost, it would remain forever as the community centrepiece just as the printer column had once stood in the dome. Sanbon spoke of returning to the wreckage, to locate Mitch's body to be buried beneath, but she would need assistance searching through the rubble, and expanding the village to raise enough shelter would be the priority at this time.

"Our hut's ready!" Hap yelled up one of the watchtowers.

Maz stood at the top, scanning the forest beyond the wall for any sign of the boy. She now understood why Mitch got so angry with him; he'd never listen and kept disappearing on little adventures and personal missions. She feared one day he would hurt himself or get lost, and nobody would hear his cry. But then he appeared, bounding through the forest swinging his Ash-bot arm, but he wasn't alone. Behind him walked a burly, hooded man, with a huge rock hammer rested on his shoulder.

The boy spotted Maz and pointed up, and the visitor raised his eyes to the tower. He was an older man, with a thick, dark grey beard and long hair. Maz recognised part of his clothing; he wore what appeared to be a ragged dome tunic, heavily stained with the colours of the forest. He stopped in the trees and waved the boy to go on ahead.

Maz hurried down the ladder, eager to learn more.

"Maz!" cried the boy as he scurried through the village gate towards her.

"Where have you been?" she asked. "And who's that man?"

"I went back to the dome," the boy replied. "He heard the blast from far away and came to look. He says he knows your name."

"How could he know my name?" Maz asked.

"His name is Max," the boy answered. "He gave you your name."

Printed in Poland
by Amazon Fulfillment
Poland Sp. z o.o., Wrocław